Desperate for Death

by

Judy Alter

Kelly O'Connell Mysteries

Copyright © 2015, Judy Alter
Desperate for Death
Media > Books > Fiction > Mystery Novels
Keywords: mystery, cozy mystery, murder, series

Digital ISBN: 978-1-62237-405-2
Digital Release: May 2015
Print ISBN 978-0-9960131-7-8

Editor, Suzanne Barrett
Cover Design by Calliope-Designs.com
Stock art by istockphotos.com

This edition is published by Alter Ego Publishing.

DEDICATION

For

Morgan and Kegan

Sawyer and Ford

Madison and Eden

Jacob

with the hope they all love books

as much as I do

Chapter One

Gus woke me. I can tell, from the depths of sleep, how serious the threat to our safety is, ranging from a scampering squirrel to someone pounding on the door. This sounded pretty serious, the barking frantic. I reached for Mike and found only an empty pillow, still warm. Alarmed, I groped for shoes and gun (Mike by now had me trained well) and rushed downstairs to the girls' bedrooms. Each slept soundly.

Then everything happened at once—the phone began to ring, I was aware of a distant alarm sound, not close enough to be the house system but perhaps the guest apartment, and through the windows of the girls' rooms, I saw the flashing red lights of emergency vehicles. Someone pounded on the front door, driving Gus even more frantic. I grabbed him and rushed for the door, forgetting that I only had on a T-shirt and underpants. Maggie would be so embarrassed when the commotion woke her!

I shut off the alarm, turned the deadbolt, and opened the door cautiously, just in case it wasn't Mike.

It wasn't, and I was glad to hide my immodesty behind the door as I looked at a uniformed firefighter. Behind him I heard shouts and yelling.

"Ma'am, is there anyone in your guest apartment? I'm afraid it's on fire."

I yelped, forgot my modesty, and nearly dropped Gus. "On fire? Seriously? No!"

Behind me, Maggie demanded, "Mom, what's going on now," her voice echoed by Em who asked more gently, "What's wrong this time?" My girls knew commotion in the middle of the night meant trouble.

Mike and I did occasionally put people in the guesthouse when they need a safe—or in one case cheap—haven, but no one had lived there for months, and we didn't go out there when it was unoccupied. I managed to tell the firefighter there was no one out there. Maggie grabbed Gus, and I closed the door in the man's face and ran for pants and shoes. It was October but darn cold outside. As I pulled on flannel pants and slid into tennis shoes, I worried about Mike. Where could he be? Grabbing a coat from the closet, I ordered the girls to stay inside and ran through the kitchen so fast I nearly missed the note on the table. I snatched it up, turned on the yard lights and ran outside, expecting the worst.

It was the worst. I could see flames through the open door of the apartment; firefighters with hoses tramped through. Whether burnt or waterlogged, everything would be ruined. And I knew enough about house fires, unfortunately, to know that they would pull all the wiring out of the ceiling. I stood and stared until Kelly Coconauer, the fire chief of the local station, put a gentle arm around my shoulders. We'd met several years ago when a property I was renovating burned. Our shared first name had made us friends.

"What happened?"

"Fellows tell me it started in the kitchen. Looks like a pan of grease caught fire. You been cooking out there? Maybe one of your girls?"

I shook my head. "No one's been out there for months. In fact, I kept thinking I should get out there and clean it thoroughly. No way there was a pan of grease on the stove."

"Good thing you didn't waste the effort cleaning it. You'll have to have it professionally repaired and cleaned now. I'll get a report to you for your records. I think they've got it under control. Structure won't be a total loss."

It looked a total loss to me, except that the walls and roof appeared untouched. I'd call Anthony, my carpenter elevated to construction manager, first thing in the morning. I remembered the note, now crumpled in my hand. I could almost read it by the outdoor lights. Thank goodness Anthony had installed them in the patio ceiling when he built the add-on to our house.

"Called out. Didn't want to wake you. Don't know how long I'll be. Love, Mike."

Mike was chief at the district police station and didn't get called out at night too often, so it must have been something big, which worried me. But in the last few years, I'd gotten used to living with a policeman who's on duty twenty-four/seven. I shoved the note in my pocket.

Just then two girls, shivering even in their coats, crept up behind me. Usually by October in Texas, temperatures were falling into the upper forties at night, but this night the predicted low was in the upper thirties and a brisk wind fanned the flames and froze the girls and me as we stood around.

"Where's Mike?" Em asked. "I'd feel better if he was here." Em relied on her stepfather for safety; clearly, she didn't think her mom provided it, since I'd gotten myself into more dangerous situations than I cared to remember.

"He got called out," I told her.

Maggie was less tentative. "Mom, you promised no more danger. You promised Mike, and you promised us."

Embarrassed that Kelly Coconauer was hearing this bit of family intimacy, I said defensively, "I didn't do anything! The apartment caught fire. We don't know how it happened. You girls go back in the house and stay there, as I told you."

Maggie turned away angrily, and after a moment Em followed her. Uselessly, I called after them, "You girls go back to bed now." They just kept walking without answering or turning to look at me. I had realized lately that I was losing my daughters, in the way all mothers lose them as they head toward their teens. They no longer thought I was right about everything, and they didn't confide in me the way they had just a year ago. I told myself family dynamics changed, and it was the nature of life.

Meanwhile, Kelly Coconauer demanded my attention. "Arson team will investigate. Unless you left grease on the stove, could be some mischief involved. And I believe you that you didn't. You're not the type to leave grease on the stove in an unoccupied guest house."

I thought back to the time Maggie hid a runaway girl in the house. Could a homeless person have moved in? There would be signs, if either the fire or the efforts to put it out didn't destroy them.

I stared at him in disbelief. "Are you kidding? Arson?" A spontaneous fire was one thing; arson was a whole different thing.

"Not ruling it out," he said.

At that moment, I would have sunk in a pile of self-pity if Mike hadn't come up the driveway at a run.

He nodded at Kelly and demanded, "What the hell is going on?"

"Fire in your guest house," Kelly said. "We'll get to the root of it."

Mike exploded. "How can there be a fire? No one's been out there in months."

Kelly just looked at him, and Mike turned to me. "Kelly, you're turning blue in the cold. Go back to bed. I'll stay out here until they wrap it up."

Usually I would have protested, but I was miserably cold and nothing sounded better than my bed. I felt a bit sick, but probably it was just the tension of wondering about the fire.

****

Next morning, Mike wanted to talk about the fire, and I wanted to throw up. Which I did, and then crawled back into bed. Mike went off to feed the girls and get them ready for school, saying he'd take them and come back. I drifted off, dreaming of burning pans of grease. When I woke up, Mike was sitting on the side of the bed.

"You okay? Did you eat something?"

I shook my head. "We all had the same thing for dinner last night...smothered steak with noodles shouldn't make anyone sick. You okay?"

"Other than tired, yeah, fine."

"It's just me. I'll get up and move slowly." And I did, but while I crept around the bedroom getting ready for the day, he questioned me.

"Kelly, I'm with Coconauer on this. It wasn't a spontaneous fire. Someone was trying to get our attention, maybe trying to get revenge. Can you think of anyone you've angered?"

I've angered! I wanted to shout what about Mike himself? He arrested people and put them in jail all the time. More likely someone would want vengeance on him. Somehow it always seemed to come back to me. But I just shook my head. Yes, I'd been involved in several major "incidents" as he called them, but most of the people who would be angry with me for those were either dead or in prison.

I countered by asking, "Why did you have to go out last night?"

"Domestic violence. A kid really, nineteen, hit his girlfriend several times, and she called 9-1-1."

"How old is she?"

"Seventeen."

"What happened?"

"He says he lost his temper. I'm not sure over what. He's just one of those punk kids who thinks he's a big power. Gave up pretty easily—all bluff and no substance—and he's cooling his heels at taxpayers' expense. She refuses to press charges. Even when her folks came to get her, she was adamant. She loves him, it was just a bad moment, and she won't file."

"Will he do time?"

"No, and he would because she's a minor. Law gets all confused at this point. Her parents could press charges, but it doesn't sound to me like they will. They were letting her live with him."

"At seventeen?" I squeaked.

"Yeah, Kelly, not everyone lives like we do. She probably dropped out of school, and I suspect she's working to support him. Now back to this fire...."

"I need to eat something," I announced.

Mike made me scrambled eggs and dry toast, bland enough to sit well on my stomach, and we both went off to our jobs without talking any more about the fire.

****

Keisha, my all-purpose assistant, was busily typing into her computer when I arrived at the office of Spencer and O'Connell. She raised an eyebrow at me but didn't speak, her way of chastising me for being late.

I am the sole owner of Spencer and O'Connell, a real estate/renovation company in the Historic Fairmount District of Fort Worth. Spencer refers to my ex-husband, but he was murdered several years ago after he had already left the girls and me and the company. I kept his name not out of sentimentality for him but because I thought O'Connell Realty sounded lame. It needed two names.

Keisha came to me from a work-study program for non-traditional students through the school district. I wouldn't have guessed it when she walked through the door, but she proved to be a gem. She appeared that first day in tight jeans, a flowing, swirling top printed with pink, purple and chartreuse, and the highest chartreuse heels I'd ever seen. I was astounded…and hesitant, but I've thanked my stars ever since that I gave her a trial run.

Today she wore a bright pink muumuu, matching heels, and her spiky hair had been tinted pink at the ends, matching her outfit and her nails, both toe and hand. She was nothing if not coordinated.

"Sorry I'm late. I wasn't feeling well this morning. Think I have a touch of a stomach bug."

"Uh-huh. I know what bug it is."

My heart sank. Keisha had sixth sense, and she usually knew things long before I did. But this time I also thought I knew what was wrong, and if she sensed it, it suddenly became gospel to me.

"We had a rough night," I said, trying to change the subject.

"Uh-huh. José goes to morning report before he meets me for breakfast. He told me about it. Any idea who set the fire?"

"No, you?"

"I got my suspicions." Changing the subject she said, "Messages for you on your desk. And the fire was in the paper…tiny little notice. Still Sheila saw it, and she's worried. You better call her."

Sheila was one of the people Mike and I had taken in for protection, especially from her televangelist husband and his goons. He was now in jail, which meant I could count him out on Mike's list of suspects. Sheila was at home in her updated Craftsman house in Fairmount, with her three-month-old baby girl, Lorna, and, I suspected, with Don Kenner, her ex-husband's former lawyer who had jumped ship at the dishonesty and unethical practices of Reverend Dr. Bruce Hollister.

I called, and even as Sheila answered I could hear the cooing soft sounds of an infant. For a moment, I was speechless, remembering those days with my girls and, frankly, longing for them again. Then, "Sheila? It's Kelly. Everything's okay. Not to worry."

"You sure? I read it might be arson, and I've been wracking my brain to think of any of Bruce's so-called followers who might have done this. Would Nick come back?"

"I doubt it." My tone was wry. Nick was a hired killer out of New York who had been sent to help Bruce Hollister—for a price, I'm sure. But the Alamo Heights police department, along with Mike, had outwitted both him and Bruce, only to have Nick post bail and jump bond within twenty-four hours. "I don't think Nick will ever set foot in Texas again or even the States. There are warrants out for him—he's probably on some tropical island that doesn't have an extradition agreement with the U.S. And Bruce has no money now to pay him. Nope, this is definitely not connected to you."

Changing the subject. "How's Lorna?" The baby was named after Sheila's late mother, Lorna McDavid, but that's another long and involved story.

"Oh, Kelly, she's the most adorable thing. Happy except when she's hungry. Loves Don and reaches for him when he comes home at night. You know how wonderful new babies are...I never knew."

"Yeah," I muttered, and my stomach did this funny flip-flop thing. We signed off, each promising to call soon. I didn't ask all the things I should have—what was Don doing these days, had he moved in, all those girl things to talk about. I wasn't in a girl-talk mood.

I waited until Keisha had gone to run errands before I called my doctor. I simply told her nurse that I hadn't been feeling well—stomach issues—and when could I get in. She scanned her calendar and said, "How about tomorrow at nine in the morning?"

"Fine," I said reluctantly. I wanted to know but I didn't. I thanked her and hung up. In less than twenty-four hours, I'd know if our lives were going to change forever. I didn't know how I felt about it. I could have gone to the drugstore and gotten one of those test kits, but I figured another twelve hours or so in denial might give me a break.

When Keisha came back, her first, oh-so-cheerful question was, "What did your doctor's office say?"

"They'll see me tomorrow."

"Well," she said with a sigh, settling down at her desk, "at least you'll know if you have a tumor." She gave a wicked little laugh.

Thank goodness the conversation was stopped by Anthony's

arrival. He blustered in, loudly complaining, "Whoever did this knows about fires, Miss Kelly. Very clever. I suppose the arson people took the pan—it wasn't there—but I doubt they'll get fingerprints. The wiring in the entire place will have to be replaced. And everything is covered with soot. You might as well chuck most of the furniture, the curtains, all that. I'll see what I can salvage. Insurance should replace wood floor, appliances, that sort of stuff. You call them yet?"

"No," I sighed. "I'm waiting for you to get me some hard figure."

"Okay. I call electrician, floor people, painters today. Structure looks sound to me. You have to figure cost of furniture. Go out there tonight and see what you can save."

That sounded depressing to me, and I sighed again.

He left, slamming the door in his lasting anger at whoever set the fire, and I sat there a bit puzzling over who that could be and why they did it. No answers popped into my mind, and a little before three, I left to go get the girls.

****

Mike was solicitous that night. Was I sure I felt all right? I assured him I did, and I was hungry. He baked potatoes, giving them a jump-start in the microwave, and fixed all kinds of toppings, including some chili from the freezer, which he seriously advised me not to eat. Of course, chili was the one thing I immediately wanted on my potato.

The girls asked about the guesthouse, and I told them Anthony was getting estimates. "He says it's major, and it will take a long time. Told me to go out there tonight and see what furniture I thought was salvageable."

"Ugh," Maggie said. "I don't want to go out there. It stinks for one thing."

"Me, neither," Em echoed.

I wished she wouldn't follow Maggie's lead in everything.

"We'll do it together, while the girls do the dishes and clean the kitchen," Mike said. "Want a jacket from the closet?"

"Yes, please."

The girls moaned and exchanged looks.

Mike brought a jacket, one for himself, and a super-duty flashlight. I noticed on the way to the guesthouse, he held my arm carefully, as though I was fragile. Immediately my mind flashed to the question: *Does he know?*

The damage was worse than I'd expected. Anthony was so right—not much if anything was salvageable. The dishes that Mrs. Hunt, the former owner, had so carefully chosen could be washed, but her lovely yellow curtains couldn't be saved. Nor as far as I could tell was any of the furniture worth restoring, though Mike claimed he or Anthony could refinish the wood desk and bookcase, both old pieces left by the Hunts. My job for the next day was to price what we'd need for replacements—a bed, chairs, appliances. The linens in the small closet were ruined and would have to be replaced. We went inside and made a list. I didn't tell Mike I had an important appointment in the morning and couldn't work on this, but I did say, "I don't think I can whip this together quickly."

He covered my hand with his and said, "It's okay, sweetheart. It doesn't have to be done right away. Just call Dave Summers and let him know it's coming, you're collecting the fire report, Anthony's estimate, and your own."

I managed a small smile. "We haven't called Dave in so long, he probably has forgotten us. I hope he doesn't think this will start another string of claims like we had when gangers vandalized my renovation project and my old house."

"He won't. But it's a good thing there's been a lapse of time."

I thought he had forgotten his inquisition about the fire and possible suspects, but when the girls were asleep and we went upstairs to our new hideaway master bedroom, he began again, though I gave him credit for trying to be subtle.

"Sweetheart, have you thought any more about who might have set the fire?"

I was ready. "No, have you thought about any of your cases? People you might have convicted, someone who is out on parole...or just plain out?"

Mike looked startled. "I'm sure it doesn't have anything to do with me. The people I come in conflict with don't know where we live, and we have an unlisted phone.

I gave him a long look. "And how hard would it be for someone on the wrong side of the law to find out where you live?"

He threw his hands up. "Okay, not hard at all. But I'm sure it's someone you tangled with in your so-called adventures. Call it instinct." He actually smirked at me.

Mike and I had an ongoing disagreement about facts versus instinct, and of course I was on the instinct side. Most of the time I'd been proven right, and he sometimes pouted. Lately he'd used instinct to twit at me.

I changed the subject. "I've had a lot on my mind, lately. I'll put Keisha on it in the morning. I have a nine o'clock appointment, so I should be in the office by ten."

"Keisha and her sixth sense?" he asked, his eyes laughing.

Mike never believed in her sixth sense, but it had saved me a couple of times, and he was slowly coming around.

As usual, Mike was sound asleep the minute he hit the bed, but my mind was on my appointment with Sherrie Goodwin the next morning. I wasn't sure why I hadn't told Mike about the looming change possible in our lives, but what if it was a false alarm? I'd see how I felt in the morning. One hand, almost of its own volition, reached for the crackers to be sure they were there. The other hand began to stroke Mike's back.

****

About three in the morning, Mike jumped out of bed, asking, "Did you hear that?"

"No," I said sleepily. "And neither did Gus. He's still asleep." The dog lay on the foot of the bed, snoring comfortingly. When Mike began to move around noisily, Gus raised his head in disapproval as if to ask, "Why are you making such a ruckus?"

I couldn't talk him into sense so Mike got dressed and went downstairs. I heard him turn off the alarm and gently open the front door. What was my wifely duty? To get the gun he insisted I have and go down as backup? Since I really hadn't heard anything—and I'm a light sleeper—I decided my duty was to stay safely in bed.

He was probably gone ten minutes when he came back upstairs and muttered sheepishly, "I didn't see anything. Nothing appears disturbed."

"Tires still have air in them?" I asked.

"Yes. And don't be sarcastic. I think that fire has me on edge."

I wanted to tell him then that he should find out who did it and stop shoving that responsibility off on me. After all, wasn't he the one who kept telling me to stay out of police business?

Chapter Two

Next morning after dropping the girls off, I stopped at the Grill for a cup of coffee and drank it slowly, staring out the window. Peter came by to refill my cup and said, "You're looking thoughtful this morning, Kelly."

"Just puzzling some things out in my mind, Peter. No more coffee, thanks."

By five minutes to nine, I was at the doctor's office. I didn't have to wait long before I was ushered into an examining room. The nurse practitioner, who introduced herself as Sally Buxton, did all those preliminaries and asked what brought me in. Mrs. Buxton wore large scrubs—she was a large woman—and had her hair pulled back in a plain style and no makeup. Clearly, she wasn't out to impress anyone. Her attitude was businesslike but also sympathetic. Yet, I thought for a moment she flashed a grin when I said I'd been feeling sick. I wasn't sure, but she was maybe fifteen years older than me, solid of build, the kind who hovers over you, taking an interest in every detail of your life, and I found myself telling her about Mike and the girls and the office and Keisha.

Dr. Goodwin, who had by now become almost a friend, was businesslike and impersonal. "Time for your annual pap, so let's see what's going on." She examined me thoroughly, then stripped off her gloves and said, "Kelly O'Connell, I'd say you're about eight weeks pregnant."

There it was. The words I knew deep down I'd hear. I couldn't tell if I should smile or sob, didn't know which I wanted to do. "Really?"

"Really. Is this a surprise?"

"Yes," I whispered. "I guess it's good news, but it…well, I hadn't planned my life around this possibility."

"How old are the girls now?" she asked.

"Fourteen and eleven."

"I can see this will be a huge change in your lives. And you're, let's see"—she flipped through the chart—"thirty-eight. Not quite an at-risk patient, but we'll watch you closely. I've got a list of instructions, but you've done this before. You know what to do. No alcohol, lots of exercise, watch the weight gain but don't starve yourself."

The familiar advice seemed to smother me.

"Gather yourself together, get dressed, and we'll talk," Sherrie Goodwin said, leaving the room.

Slowly I put my clothes back on, stopping to rub my belly in that age-old gesture of comforting the little one inside. I took extra care with my hair and repairing my make-up, such as it was, and then I sat for a long time in that straight, uncomfortable chair that is found in all examining rooms. My mind rolled around the to-do list I now faced—mostly telling people. Eight weeks was early—I'd always held my breath until twelve weeks, knowing that miscarriage was a possibility. I supposed even more so at my age.

But I couldn't, wouldn't, didn't want to hide this from Mike…or the girls. And once they knew, the cat was out of the bag. Keisha would know, probably already knew from the way she'd been talking. And my mom—I was sure Cynthia O'Connell would be embarrassed by her daughter's wanton behavior. Anthony would say, "Children are God's gift. God is good." I could hear them all in my head. Claire, who'd had a life of trial with husbands and children and was now my best friend, after a rocky start, would understand my joy mixed with qualms.

Dr. Goodwin didn't come back in herself but sent Mrs. Buxton, who apologized that Dr. Goodwin had gotten caught up with a semi-emergency with a patient. I wondered what a semi-emergency was but didn't really mind. "Ms. O'Connell, I can imagine this is a big surprise. But we'll support you every way we can. And you don't need that lecture about the blessings of a second family. You'll find that out for yourself. Here's a list of vitamins we recommend, plus an over-the-counter medication that should help with morning sickness."

She watched me for a minute, as I glanced at the paperwork, and then she asked, "Any questions?"

I shook my head, and she said, "Good. I'll probably be the one to see you most of the time, so here's my card. Call if you have questions or get worried. I'm looking forward to going through this pregnancy with you."

Actually I felt reassured by her attitude and what I perceived as her capability. I left, making my next appointment for a month later as instructed.

As soon as I was in the car, I called Mike. "Meet me for lunch at Lili's?"

He chuckled. "Sure, what's the occasion? We usually have lunch at the Grill or Mona's Bun Appetit."

"This is a special occasion," I said. "See you there about 11:15, before it gets crowded?"

"You got it," and he hung up.

I went to the office, where Keisha eyed me sidewise and asked, "You sell a house this morning?"

"Not quite," I said. Then, in a rush, "I've got a couple good prospects." I'd been thinking about both enlarging the scope of my agency and transferring more responsibility to Keisha. Somehow, in those wakeful nights, I'd concluded we ought to manage rental properties and that Keisha could manage that end of the business. To forestall other questions about my morning, I decided to discuss that right now.

When I presented my idea, she said, "Good thinking, Kelly. It would work for us."

"You want to scout the neighborhood for likely properties?" I asked. "Some will need Anthony's fine touch before we can rent them, and he's tied up for now on the guest house. But keep an eye out for ones that we can rent right now and ones that will need work." I told her I'd pay a commission out of the rental income, after we figured expenses against income and projected recovery. That took her back a bit, but she said, "Sure. Thanks."

I thought I was off the hook for any questions her sixth sense might suggest.

Not much later, I left for Lili's. It was just four blocks from my office, both the office and the restaurant on Magnolia Avenue, and I figured I best get used to walking for exercise. I coached myself to put on a cheerful face, reminding myself that I was delivering good news. Mike was waiting in the crowded entryway when I got there. He kissed me gently and led me to the table that he'd requested, in the annex where it was more quiet.

When we were seated, he ignored the menu and asked directly,

"So what's up?"

No sugarcoating. I told him, "You're going to be a father...again. We're expecting."

Mike doesn't swear often but now he said, loudly, "Holy shit! Are you serious?"

I looked around to make sure no one had heard his outburst, and then I took his hand and said, "Yeah, I'm sure. So is Dr. Goodwin."

"Want a glass of wine to celebrate?"

I shook my head. "I can't. Not for another seven months or so."

He almost said "Holy shit!" again. But then he reached for my hand, grasping it in both of his. "I know this will be hard on you...harder than I can even imagine. But I have to say I'm excited." He paused and then stammered on, "I love the girls with all my heart. You know that. But the idea of my own baby...."

I pulled my hand loose and put a finger to his mouth. "Our baby," I said. "Something we created together."

Mike Shandy actually got up from the table, walked around it, and pulled me up into a huge bear hug and a passionate kiss. People at the next table clapped, and I heard one say, "I want what she's having." That old line from *When Harry Met Sally*.

Vance, the owner, came by and asked, "Champagne in order? I know you guys are married, but there's obviously something to celebrate."

'Water for her," Mike said, "and a Samuel Adams for me."

It wasn't exactly a festive celebration, but we did have grilled tilapia. And as we ate, we got down to nuts and bolts—with telling the girls at the top of the list. Mike well knew my increasing worries about my relationship with the girls, and the idea of breaking this news to them scared the daylights out of me.

"Mike, they know what it takes to make a baby. They'll look at us like, 'You two did that?'"

"No they won't. They know we love each other, and if we have to we'll explain that's what married couples in love do."

I sighed. With high school nearly upon us and frightening statistics out there about sexually active high school students, I didn't think we were setting a good example.

Mike exploded at that. "Are we supposed to have a platonic marriage? You're comparing apples and oranges! They're nothing the same."

We finally decided we would take the girls to dinner—not the Grill, not Bun Appetit, not even Lili's. We'd go to the new pizza place they'd been clamoring to try. I crossed my fingers it wouldn't be too noisy.

"And after that," Mike said, "we'll have a family dinner this Sunday, invite everyone, and get it all over with at once."

I couldn't at that point tell him about my twelve-week rule. I just said a silent prayer for the child in my belly.

****

Em was delighted by the idea of real pizza in a restaurant and not the stuff that came to your door in a greasy cardboard box. "I want hamburger and pepperoni and cheese and olives and, oh, I don't know what else," she said, dancing around the room.

Maggie was a bit more suspicious. "It's a school night. Why are we going?"

Mike shrugged. "I know you girls want to try it, and your mom's kind of tired tonight. No need to make her stand in the kitchen. You rather go to the Grill?"

Maggie shook her head. "No, I want pizza. Just wondered."

When we were seated in the rustic restaurant, all of Maggie's suspicions apparently vanished. We were all carried away with Italian terms for which we had no translation and had to have serious conversations with our waiter. Mike and I could explain caprese and focaccia and antipasti (Em thought it was spelled wrong) but even we were puzzled by *soppressata* or the difference between prosciutto crudo and prosciutto *cotto*. Em was dismayed that the menu had sausage but no pepperoni pizza—the waiter found her a near substitute. Mike had the meatball sandwich, and Maggie followed his lead. Much aware of my new physical state, I had a large salad with all the things whose names I didn't know. We all stuck with familiar tiramisu for dessert.

Maggie was eyeing us again. "Dessert? Fancy dessert? What's up with you guys tonight?"

We smiled and made a big production of holding hands at the table, which made her say, laughingly, "Oh, cut that out."

"I tell you what. Let's take our tiramisu to go and have it at home. We'll have a party." Mike beamed with pleasure at his idea. "It's pretty noisy in here."

Maggie still looked doubtful, but that's just what we did. While the girls changed into pajamas, Mike crafted a party with sparkling white grape juice for the girls and me and white wine for him, which made me a tad jealous. I was tired and wine would have tasted so good. Mike was right—I was exhausted, maybe just thinking about what lay ahead.

The girls returned together, and while Em squealed at the sparkling juice—she still called it "kid wine"—Maggie said, "Okay, what gives?"

Mike got a bit pompous. "We're going to have an addition to the family."

"A cat," Em yelled. "You're getting me a cat!"

Maggie gave her a disgusted look and then turned toward us. "Are you telling me you're going to have a baby?"

Mike nodded.

And Maggie said the last thing I wanted to hear. "How embarrassing. Everyone will know what you've been doing."

We were both speechless, until Mike finally said, "We're married, Maggie. That's what married couples do."

Em jumped in with, "Can you make it a girl? I want another sister." Then she was quick to hug Maggie and say, "Because I like the one I have so much. I don't know if a boy would fit in around here."

"Will I have to babysit?" Maggie asked.

And then they were both off with a thousand questions, and we talked plans—where the baby would sleep, things like that.

When we finally sent them off to bed, Maggie said, "I guess if you're happy about it, I am too. It will probably be fun to have a baby. I...I just didn't know people had them at your age."

Which left both of us speechless again.

****

The next morning, the girls and I rushed out to my car, running a bit late for school. There, propped against the tire under the gas tank, was a half-empty bag of sugar. Some had poured out into a little pile, which the ants were busily attacking. I knew all the horror stories about sugar caramelizing in the engine and gunking it up so badly the only thing to do was replace it.

I groaned. "My car's ruined." Then, more decisively, "Em, run get Mike. He'll have to take you girls to school."

Mike, bless him, came at a run, and I began shouting as he hit the door. "My car's ruined. Sugar in the gas tank."

"Probably not. That's an urban legend. It may gum up the filter. First thing to do is drain the tank and see if there really is any sugar in the gas." Then, turning to the girls, "Get in my car." And he backed out of the driveway as fast as he dared.

I called Anthony, who was on his way to work on the guesthouse anyway. He shook his head and said, almost to himself, "Who does this kind of things? Sometimes, Miss Kelly, they leave the sugar as a kind of bad prank. I'll go get a bucket and drain the tank, see if there really is sugar in it."

I was reassured that he and Mike had the same approach. He got an empty garbage can out of the shed, and I watched fascinated as Anthony siphoned the gas out of the tank, praying he didn't get any in his mouth as he sucked to get the suction going. He seemed to know exactly what he was doing, and soon gas was flowing into the garbage can. Thank heaven I hadn't just filled the tank, and it was at most half-empty.

Mike came back and peered into the garbage can but I thought it too dark to tell anything. Both men stared at the steady stream of gas.

"Wouldn't it all sink to the bottom of the tank?" I asked tentatively.

"Not necessarily," Mike said. "Sugar doesn't dissolve in gas, and this should stir it up. I don't see anything. Did you try to start the car?"

I shook my head.

Mike threw up his hands, while Anthony hid a grin. "If you don't try to start it, you don't know if any damage has been done."

"What if I do start it and it kills the engine forever?"

Mike rolled his eyes and cast a sideways glance at Anthony, who tactfully looked away. "It won't, Kelly, trust me." They poured a portion of the gas into a clear glass container—had Mike really gotten my water pitcher from the kitchen?—and held it up to the light. Even I could tell the liquid looked clear. With a large funnel, they poured the gas back into the tank and ordered me to start my car. I wasn't sure if it would explode and blow me to smithereens or exactly what would happen, but I climbed in, took a deep breath, and turned the key. The engine balked, the sound it makes when it doesn't have enough gas.

"Keep it in park and hit the gas," Mike called.

This time, with a vision of speeding through the guesthouse wall, I did as he told me, and the engine caught and purred.

Mike walked up to the driver's window, leaned in to kiss me and said, "We'll talk about this tonight. Who knows? Maybe one of Maggie's friends was pranking you."

I knew that wasn't true. This was the kind of thing that boys did, not girls, and Maggie didn't have friends of the opposite gender, at least not who knew me well enough to pull this kind of prank.

All the way to the office, I clung nervously to the steering wheel, half expecting the car to stall in the middle of a street. You'd think I was driving twenty miles, but it was less than a five-minute drive on back streets. With a sigh of relief, I pulled in behind our building and stumbled into the office.

Keisha glanced up at me and then, deliberately, at the clock. She looked at me again and must have seen how pale I was. "You okay?"

"Car trouble," I said lamely and explained about the bag of sugar.

"At least it's not as bad as setting the guesthouse on fire." She got up and poured me a cup of coffee. Keisha was a gem, because she honestly didn't feel diminished by serving coffee.

"But it's a pattern," I said. "Someone's out to get me again. I'm tired of being chased."

"I'm gonna figure it out, Kelly. You just relax and take care of that baby. Now, let's talk about something brighter. How did the girls take your news?"

It dawned on me I'd never told her about the baby. When I came back from a long lunch with Mike, she was out driving the neighborhood looking for rental properties. Her sixth sense had kicked in all along, and she knew. But the girls' reaction wasn't exactly a bright subject with which to begin talking about my pregnancy.

"Not with unbounded joy. Em thought we were getting her a kitten, and Maggie was a bit embarrassed. But they began to come around. I think outfitting a nursery and buying baby clothes will draw them into it. I hope."

"It will," she said confidently.

Sometimes I wished she wasn't so darn smug about that sixth sense.

Once I settled down to business, I was all efficiency. "Keisha, let's talk about rental properties some more. Want to drive me around to see the ones you spotted yesterday?" I think she was disappointed I wouldn't just let her offer a contract sight unseen, but that wasn't the way I did things.

"Sure," she said. "I didn't just fix on houses with For Sale signs but picked some that were poorly kept. I figured the owners weren't interested in the house, and if we could get one cheap enough, Anthony could fix it up for a rental."

Keisha knew I didn't miss her use of the pronoun, "we," instead of "you." She was making herself a partner in the business. As well she should. Except that it would require a bit of ego-squelching for me. *Kelly, you have a lot on your plate—a new baby, a possible stalker. You need Keisha to take more responsibility.* My other side argued, *Okay, as long as she knows I make the final decisions.*

Keisha gave me a long look, and I knew she read the thoughts going through my mind. Neither of us said a word.

So we drove—Keisha knew better than to choose the ramshackle duplexes that I thought should be on the demolition list. She had spotted five houses—two of those contemporary red brick small bungalows with garages opening to the street, that now peppered the neighborhood. They were newly enough built that I thought they'd be in reasonable condition if the tenants hadn't trashed them. Two others were modest frame houses that I would like to renovate but I couldn't afford to do that to every house in Fairmount—still they would need a fair amount of work before I'd lease them. The final one—which I knew she saved for last—was a charmingly redone Craftsman. Small, it featured horizontal boarding painted a pale yellow with moss green trim on windows, door and the covered porch. Organza curtains hung in the windows.

"Young couple lives here, and they adore the house. But his business is sending him to England for two years. They want to lease but have it to come back to. I didn't know if you wanted to get into property management…but if you do, I think José and I might move into this one. That apartment of mine is gettin' awful small." Eyes straight ahead, she didn't look at me as she said this. "That is, after we get married!"

I screeched so loud she almost ran into a parked car.

Chapter Three

Keisha concentrated on her driving, eyes on the road, not looking at me. But she said, "Kelly O'Connell, don't you tell a soul. José don't know about this yet."

At that all thoughts of a new baby, sugar in my gas tank, and the burned guesthouse flew out of my mind, and I hooted. "What? When are you going to tell him?"

She was unperturbed. "That boy is as good as gold, but he's not much on coming up with new ideas. I have to sort of coax him along."

The thought flittered through my brain that we might have a joint announcement party Sunday night—our baby and the engagement of Keisha and José, but I guess the latter was out of the question.

"So when's the wedding?"

She never hesitated. "When's your baby due?"

"Late May, early June," I said, wondering what this had to do with the price of eggs.

"Well, we got to get married well before that, so you can host a shower. I want a big, fancy do, with all the trimmings."

She was not embarrassed about announcing what she wanted, and I quickly figured Claire would help me. Claire was the world's best hostess.

We arrived back at the office, settled in our chairs, and discussed rental properties. I decided on one of the new brick houses and one of the redo ones. The current tenants could stay until Anthony was ready to work on it, when he finished the guesthouse—which was progressing slowly. Then I told Keisha she ought to lease the Craftsman she wanted but only if there was a provision for lease-to-buy if the owners' long-range plans changed. It happens. And I'd advise her on writing that into the lease. I supposed José's opinion didn't count.

"When are the owners moving?" I asked.

"Not till April," Keisha said smugly. "It will all work out fine." She had this figured out long before she told me, and I wondered how she knew the house was available. It didn't have a For Lease sign in the yard. Yes, I thought we should go into property management, but not with that house. It should be Keisha's own private deal.

We worked together on figures, and I told her to make offers to buy the two we decided on. Then I turned my attention to the announcement party Sunday night, making a list of people. It was so chilly these days that instead of asking people to bring things and making poor Mike stand out in the cool night grilling hamburgers, I decided to make a big pot of chili. Well, maybe it would take two pots, but we could do it. I'd need someone to make the second pot of chili, two people to make cornbread, and two or three to make a salad. These days, since we'd taken Sheila and Don into the fold, there were twenty-one of us. Cooking was getting out of hand.

When I went out to my car to get the girls from school, I smelled the strong odor of gasoline but didn't see anything. Tried to start the car, but the gas gauge flashed that red "Empty" alert at me. Hadn't Mike and Anthony put all the gas back in my car? I wish I could say logic made me walk around the car but it was just puzzlement. But there, on the other side, under the gas tank door, was a large wet puddle—gasoline. It ran toward the street in small rivulets.

Furious I stalked back into the office and asked Keisha to get the girls. Then I called Anthony, who said he'd fill a gas can and come as quickly as he could. Then I threw the phone book—the first thing that my hand touched—hard against the wall. Glad it wasn't my iPhone or something breakable.

Having vented myself, I sat down and gave in to tears—not bawling but tears running down my face, sniffles of self-pity.

And the office door opened and Claire walked in. One look at me and she demanded, "What the hell is going on?"

I wiped my face with a tissue and said, "You wouldn't believe it."

"Tell me." She planted herself in my visitor's chair.

I shook my head. "I'll tell you most of it Sunday night. We're having a potluck dinner. You don't have a date, do you?"

"I do now. With you."

"Good." I hiccupped. "Can you bring a big batch of cornbread?"

She shrugged. "Sure. I make great cornbread, lots of sugar. But I don't think I can wait until Sunday."

Just then, Keisha and the girls came in. "Claire," Em said delightedly, "have you heard Mom's news? Well, I guess it's Mom and Mike's news together."

Claire raised an eyebrow at me. "No, sweetie, I haven't, but I don't think you're supposed to tell me. I have to wait until we all have Sunday dinner."

That totally distracted Em. "Are we having everybody for dinner?" She clapped her hands when I nodded.

The thought of the dinner was already beginning to make me tired, and I was weary of secrets.

"Can I tell, Mom? Can I? Please?" I nodded, and she burst forth with, "Mom's going to have another baby!"

If Claire hadn't already been sitting down, she would have fallen. Her jaw fell open; she gripped the arms of her chair and stared at me. "Really?"

"Would I make that up?"

Claire was the one person who knew not to do an instantaneous dance of joy. "You okay with it?"

I nodded. "Not at first, but I am now. I'm beginning to get excited. It's just…there's so much else."

At which propitious moment Anthony barged in the door with his gasoline can. "Mike said to wait until they can try for fingerprints," he announced loudly.

While Claire said, "What's going on?"

Keisha said, "Get that thing out of here, old man. You want to burn us all up."

He gave Keisha a dirty look and went to put the can in the parking lot.

"I'll tell you, Aunt Claire," Maggie said with a weary tone. "Mom's done it again. Somebody's stalking her. That's why our guesthouse burned."

So there we were—Claire looking less put together and sophisticated than usual, Keisha still miffed at Anthony, the girls uncertain, and me on the verge of tears—in short we were all a mess. And just then, a well-dressed youngish man walked in—looked like a banker to me. Suit, conservative tie, polished shoes, briefcase in one hand. His hair, brown without a trace of gray, had been expensively cut. I pegged him at thirty-five at the most.

He took in the scene for a long, silent moment and then managed to say, "I'm looking for Kelly O'Connell. Have I…have I come to the right place?"

I brushed the tissue over my face again, rose from my seat and held out my hand. "You have. I'm Kelly O'Connell. How can I help you?"

Claire quietly vacated the visitor's chair, going to sit by Keisha, and I invited the gentleman to sit down. His hands, as he fingered his briefcase, were long, delicate, and pale. I figured he either worked at a desk all the time or played a musical instrument. He definitely did no physical labor, and I doubted he worked out much.

"I represent the law firm of Bachman and Bannister," he said, deftly whipping out a card that he had obviously had up his sleeve the whole time.

I read the card. His name was Benjamin Cruze and though the card didn't say it, I surmised that he was a junior partner in this lofty law firm. "What can I do for you?" I asked, now thoroughly puzzled.

"We represent the late Robert Martin, and you are named in his will." Once again, his movements were smooth as he pulled out a letter, this time from the inside pocket of his suit coat. "I thought it best to deliver this in person."

It was a formal letter informing me that I was left a bequest of one half of the estate of Robert Martin. I read it twice and then raised my eyes to him in utter confusion. "Why me? I don't think I know Mr. Martin…er, knew him."

"He's left you this generous bequest for the education fund of your daughters...."

I wanted to ask what education fund, because one thing I worried about was that neither Mike nor I had the wherewithal to put aside college money for the girls.

"Why would he leave me money?"

He cleared his throat, and his hand tapped nervously on his briefcase. "Ummm, it's a bit irregular, but he is Jo Ellen North's father."

Jo Ellen North! The woman who had killed my ex-husband and tried her damnedest to kill me. Of course. It all came back to me now. Jo Ellen was serving a long prison sentence at the women's penitentiary in Gatesville. I knew the very mention of her adored father leaving me money would send her ballistic. Last I knew he was a broken man, his murdering wife in last stages of Alzheimer's and he himself so frail, after living through his daughter's trial, that he required twenty-four-hour care.

Benjamin Cruze went on, his monotone voice never changing inflection. "With guards, paid for by the family, Mrs. North was allowed to see her father before he died and then, later, to attend the private memorial service. She was...." He paused, apparently searching for the words to put it delicately, "upset that you had been remembered in her father's will. She claims you ruined his life and, of course, hers, since she's imprisoned."

"But won't the bulk of his estate go to her?"

"Only the remainder after your half and a few minor bequests, and that in a trust until, if and when, she is released. It will be invested for her. Our law firm will manage the account. She will get a small monthly allowance for things she needs to purchase in the penitentiary—whatever personal clothing is allowed, stationery, things like that. But there's no guarantee she'll ever see the rest of the money."

"Is it an enormous amount of money? I…I can't accept it. Can I just refuse and forfeit the money?" *Sorry, Maggie and Em, but you'll have to earn scholarships.*

"Yes, you can disclaim the money. It will revert to charities, although I cannot tell you what charities. Martin specified the entire trust would not revert to his daughter. I guess he suspected you'd do something like that, but remember, he wanted you to have the money."

I was floored. Why would Robert Martin leave me money? In trying to identify a skeleton found in a house I was renovating, I followed lead after lead until I found that Martin's wife, Jo Ellen's mother, had killed her husband's pregnant lover, and Jo Ellen had witnessed the murder when she was a young child. Jo Ellen didn't much care about her mother, but she was fiercely protective of her father, which is what led her to try to kill me…in front of my girls. But it was now old history—six years old at least. And Robert Martin had to face the secret he'd hidden for so many years. His wife was then already in the advanced stages of Alzheimer's and died soon after.

"Why? Robert Martin and his family had reason to hate me. I…ah, uncovered the skeleton in their background. Quite literally."

Cruze had an answer ready. "Mr. Martin's message with the bequest says it is a way of thanking you for helping an old man live with his conscience."

I could feel my color rising, right along with my anxiety. This couldn't be real. My hands grew clammy, my heart beat rapidly, and my head felt light. I managed to sound calm as I said, "I…I can't think about this anymore right now, Mr. Cruze. Thank you for coming to see me. I'll be in touch." I stood by way of dismissal and offered my hand.

He understood. "Of course. I know this is hard to comprehend. I'll wait to hear from you. Thank you for seeing me."

My one rational thought, as he left the office, was that he was a corporation twit, with a lot of good manners and not a clue about people in the real world. I fingered the business card he had left in my hand.

Claire, Keisha, and both my girls sat spellbound and quiet, but the minute Mr. Big Money Lawyer was out the door they exploded.

"That Jo Ellen North may work herself into apoplexy before she ever gets any of her daddy's money," Keisha announced, with no small amount of glee.

Maggie was erupting with a joyful shout! "College money! I can go anywhere I want." She danced a jig around the office, but Em was less exuberant. "Do we have to use it for college? Could we use it for the new baby?"

I hugged my sweet girl. "I don't think we'll use it for anything, girls. I don't feel right about taking it." My mind jumped to Mike. He would know what to do. I wanted to see him this minute, but I doubted he'd make himself available at three-thirty in the afternoon. I'd have to wait until supper. "Girls, let's go home and get you started on homework, while I fix supper."

Claire gently reminded me that I hadn't been cleared to drive my car. Mike apparently hadn't dusted it for prints, and Anthony's gas can still sat outside the back of the office. So she offered to drive us home, which is what happened.

Grumbling, the girls headed for Claire's car, and I called over my shoulder that Keisha should come for supper after she closed the office. "I thought you'd never ask," she said. Claire, on the other hand, declined, saying she wanted to fix dinner for her daughters and would hear all about what was decided Sunday night.

"It won't," I said with a touch of bitterness, "be a part of the news of the celebration evening." *Of all the bad timing for Robert Martin to leave me money now when I was focused on a new baby!* Then I dismissed that as a selfish thought. He probably didn't want to die whenever he had, and that was worse than my inconvenience.

Supper was unimaginative. Tuna casserole, though I did have a killer recipe that everyone liked—it involved boiling dried herbs in wine and adding to the traditional mushroom soup base of the casserole. And because I was tired of salads, I put out a plate of raw veggies with a homemade ranch dip. Everyone ate heartily, but they all had one eye on me as Mike went around the table asking how everyone's day was.

"Kelly?"

"Ah…I had an unusual day…."

"I know about your car," he said with just a bit of impatience, "We dusted it. No fingerprints. Anthony filled it with gas, and you're good to go tomorrow. Since your car is still at the office, I'll drive the girls to school and you to the office. Anything else?"

"Oh tell him, Mom." Maggie was bouncing in her seat so much that Mike gave her one of his long "table manners" looks.

The story spilled out, with Keisha here and there supplying a detail I'd forgotten. When we both wound down, Mike pushed his chair from the table, went to get himself another beer, sat back and down, and said, "Wow!"

"What do you think?" I asked.

He shook his head. "I have no idea. What do you think?"

"I think I want to disclaim the money."

He looked long and hard at me. "Why? We don't have a college fund for the girls or for Snickerdoodle"—that was his new name for the baby I was carrying.

"But it's blood money," I protested. "It's got Marie Winton's blood all over it." Marie was Robert Martin's lover who at six months pregnant and happily planning for her child was shot and killed by Robert Martin's wife. "I can't take it."

Mike responded slowly and deliberately. "Robert Martin didn't leave you the money as blackmail. As that young lawyer told you, he left it out of gratitude. Maybe you should think of it as victim compensation. You were a victim, after all, and so were your girls who lost their father."

That made both girls startle, and Mike looked at them and said, "Girls, Tim Spencer was your father, no matter the relationship, and you deserve compensation for growing up without a father."

"We have a father, Mike. You." Em folded her arms across her chest and got on her obstinate look.

Mike grinned—he couldn't help it. "Thank you. But the principle remains the same. You were robbed of your father. And your mother was almost killed. Robert Martin was, in my opinion, truly trying to make amends." He paused a minute, lost in thought. "I never met Mr. Martin, but I've certainly heard enough about him. He was a rich man with some unsavory connections and I'm not sure he always walked on the side of the law. But on the other hand, I know he was prominent in society in this city and generous in his donations to charities he cared about. I think this is an example of his generosity. And he's not here for us to question him."

Chapter Four

Mike was not quite so cavalier about the inheritance when we were tucked in the privacy of our bedroom—the tree suite he called it, since it was elevated above the rest of the house and surrounded by old trees. "Kelly, that inheritance worries me."

I flared in anger. "That's not what you said at the dinner table."

"Hear me out." He raised a palm in the peace gesture. "I think you should accept the money. It's due you. But have you thought about how furious this must have made Jo Ellen North?"

I shrugged. "Not really. She's locked up. She can't do anything."

"You'd be surprised at what plans prisoners can hatch and see carried out. Does she have any siblings?"

"I'm pretty sure not...and that Benjamin Cruze didn't mention any. The other half of the estate will be held in trust for Jo Ellen, provided she ever gets out of prison, and minus a few charitable bequests."

"I don't suppose she will ever see it. But Martin was philanthropically generous, so I imagine many charities could benefit. But I wish we could find out about siblings. That may be the clue to who's harassing you."

I bristled a bit because, in my mind, we still weren't sure it wasn't someone harassing Mike, some ex-con with a powerful grudge. "I don't think Jo Ellen's reach extends that far."

"You underestimated her before, and it almost cost you your life."

I had a flashback to that afternoon when Jo Ellen and I fought like tigers over the gun she had aimed at me. If it hadn't been for the girls distracting her and Theresa, Anthony's daughter who was babysitting that afternoon, finally grabbing the gun as it skittered across the floor, I have no doubt I'd be dead. I'd fought hard, something I'd never done before in my life, but I underestimated Jo Ellen's determination and her physical strength. The memory still made me shaky.

"I don't want to think about it," I said and climbed into bed, turning my back to him. Behind me, I heard Mike sigh. And I think it was one of the few nights he didn't go right to sleep. I was well aware of his restless movements beside me.

The next morning I called Mr. Cruze, told him I would accept the money, but I wanted it to go to a trust fund, and I would call him with details after the fund was established. Then I made an appointment at Claire's bank.

****

By Sunday I had put Jo Ellen and inheritances and harassment out of my mind. I spent most of the morning in the kitchen making chili for the multitudes. I had purchased disposable soup bowls and plates. I care as much about the environment as the next person but with more than twenty people to feed, I knew I wasn't going to have the energy to hand wash those dishes. Mike was often after me to install a dishwasher, and he didn't listen to my argument that they weren't authentic to Craftsman houses. Today a part of me longed for that dishwasher. It took two slow-cookers to hold all the chili I made, and I was briefly glad Mike and I had each brought a cooker to the marriage.

People began drifting in about five-thirty and by six everyone was there except Claire's older daughter, Megan, and her boyfriend, Brandon. It was too chilly to be outside as I anticipated, and I wondered about the wisdom of serving chili to people who were going to have to eat out of their laps, but it was too late to do anything about it.

Mike rapped a table knife on his beer bottle and said, "If I could have your attention a moment...."

Heads turned toward him; curious people drifted out of the kitchen. Em and Keisha beamed in anticipation, but Maggie looked at the floor and would not return my smile. Most others looked puzzled. Mike rarely made speeches, before or after dinner. He motioned for me to stand beside him, so I did, carrying my glass of sparkling cider. I was afraid I was even getting to like the sweet stuff.

"Kelly and I want to share a piece of good news with you. We are going to have another baby."

I don't know what I expected, but I wasn't prepared for the total silence that took over for more than a minute. Then the room exploded into a cacophony of questions and exclamations. When was it due? (Probably late May.) Boy or girl? (We didn't know.) Would I keep working? (Yes, but Keisha would take more responsibility—she beamed at that.) What did the girls think? (Let them speak for themselves—though Maggie's expression told me she still had doubts, to say the least.) Mostly, though, it was a joyful response. The downer comment came, predictably, from my mom. Cynthia O'Connell sidled up to me and said, "Sweetie, aren't you a little old? I mean, is it safe? You know how I worry about you."

"Mom," I whispered, "I'm not forty yet. Don't worry. Let me do that. You take care of Otto."

Maggie's best friend, Jenny, had come with her mom, Mona. Ever since they were freed from the abusive domination of Mona's husband and Jenny's dad, who dealt drugs, they were different people—happy in their new small apartment and very close to each other. Jenny often worked at Bun Appetit, the small haute dog restaurant Mona had opened.

I saw Maggie pull Jenny aside after they got their chili and head back into the bedroom wing where they would no doubt trade confidences. I longed to be a fly on the wall, but I feared I wouldn't like what I heard. Maggie would complain about the embarrassment of having a pregnant mom at her age and about the danger I put everyone into.

Sheila, who was so entranced by her three-month-old, was indignant that I didn't tell her when we talked a few days ago, but she quickly forgot indignation as she cooed to little Lorna about having a playmate just her age. I figured they'd be about a year apart in age.

Everyone else was milling about, helping themselves to chili and cornbread. Mona pulled me aside to whisper, "Maggie told Jenny about the baby a couple of days ago. I hope you don't mind, but Jenny was so excited…and more than a little bit jealous."

Startled, I whispered, "What did Maggie say?"

"I don't exactly know, but Jenny said she told Maggie she ought to be a lot more excited than she is."

"Maggie's embarrassed that…you know…Mike and I had sex at our advanced ages," I said, trying to keep bitterness out of my tone.

Mona just laughed aloud.

The rest of the evening people treated me as if I was fragile. "Now, Kelly, you just sit down and put your feet up." "Can I bring you more chili?" "Here, let me take your bowl so you don't have to get up." Without even realizing it, I found myself pushed into Otto's favorite chair, while he sat on the couch and stared at me, with Mom patting his knee as though to say, "There, there, it will be all right."

Claire drifted by and commented, "Enjoy it while you can. I foresee rough days ahead." Little did she know the truth of it!

Mike came by, kissed the top of my head, and said, "You're the princess tonight…and well you should be."

Keisha and Mom did dishes, refusing to let me help, and I thought it was probably good for them to renew their friendship. Mom had been definitely hesitant when we announced Keisha would move in with her during the period a serial killer was targeting older women in Fairmount. Keisha had bullied and cajoled her until they became friends, and to this day Keisha looked out for the woman she called "Miss Cynthia."

I sat, feet in the chair, perfectly relaxed, and let the evening swirl around me. At one point Em came up, hugged me, planted a big kiss on my cheek, and ran off again to do something with Anthony's sons. It was a lovely family gathering, and I was grateful beyond measure.

When they all left, my kitchen was clean, leftovers put away, the world in order. The girls went to bed without being told, and I collapsed into our bed. Mike joined me almost immediately and wrapped his arms around me, stroking my hair. I fell asleep almost instantly and slept soundly the entire night.

****

Life went predictably on, and there was no harassment for over a week. I began to get complacent, but I knew Keisha was watching me every moment. I brushed it off. If she made me too nervous, I'd speak to her.

On Tuesday afternoon, Claire called. "I'm desperate," she said, and I could tell from her voice that she was. "My boss is giving me trouble, the guy I went out with Saturday night thinks he's a fixture in my life, and I'm worried about Megan…well, I need to vent and rant. Can you leave Mike and the kids for supper tonight? My treat."

"Let me call Mike," I said. I did, and he agreed that if Claire needed me, I should go to supper.

"Be careful though. Be aware of your surroundings. Got your gun with you?"

"Yes," I muttered, almost resentfully.

I called Claire back, and we tried to think of someplace quiet where we could talk without shouting and without being overheard. That ruled out most of the places we usually went until I remembered a small Greek place on Seventh Street. It was BYOB and the food was good. The only thing was that it was closed as often as it was open. Claire agreed to experiment and bring a bottle of white wine, if I would call. Success—it was open, and we set off about six. I drove and picked her up, so she could help me navigate the dark and roughly paved parking lot. When she poured wine, I reminded her I couldn't drink.

"Oh, damn. That's right. Sorry if I drink in front of you."

I assured her it was all right.

Claire did have a lot on her mind. She began her rant with the conviction that her oldest daughter, Megan, was sleeping with her boyfriend.

"Claire, she's what? A junior in college? Twenty years old,

dating this boy how long? Do you really expect her to be a virgin at her wedding? Were you?"

"No, but that's different…" She paused and stared off into space. "I guess it's not, is it? But I want her to have a happy marriage, not like my spotty record."

"Then trust her, keep her your friend, and don't set down unrealistic rules. Megan's a great girl."

"What if she gets pregnant like I did?"

"I think girls these days are pretty savvy about that." I realized in telling her not to worry I was shoveling out advice I probably didn't take myself. I worried about everything! And I was worrying about losing Maggie, when she was only fourteen. Maybe I was putting the cart before the horse or bringing my bridges up to jump them or whatever other cliché you can think of.

"Okay, but call me when Maggie's twenty…." she said, as though she read my thoughts.

"Tell me about the man Saturday night," I said, anxious to change the subject.

Before she could answer, our dolma and *saganaki* arrived. I loved that Greek cheese, doused with lemon and then flamed at the table. We both dug in.

Finally, she said, "He's a surgeon, and just what you'd expect from a surgeon. Thinks he's God's gift to women and was offended that I didn't tumble into bed with him that night. I think he sees a woman as a reflection of him."

No wonder she's worried about Megan. She's worried about herself. "Well, be flattered that he thinks you're good-looking enough to reflect well on him when you're on his arm."

"I avoided his arm. In fact, toward the end of the evening I avoided eye contact. We had dinner at Grace downtown—lovely, elegant, I even had Steak Diane. But it was the most boring evening of my life."

"So?" I prompted.

"He's called twice a day Sunday and Monday. I've gotten so I look at caller ID and don't answer, or I have one of the girls tell him I'm not in. But I think he's one of those men who sees a reluctant woman as a challenge."

I couldn't help but laugh aloud, which turned heads toward me. In my single days, I'd never ever had such a problem. Most men never called twice. It's one of the reasons I treasure Mike—he apparently saw something other men didn't, beyond the curly hair, lack of style, too much weight, and a tendency to be curious and tenacious. Wait? Is that my self-image? Must work on that. I drew my thoughts back to Claire.

"Just answer one time. Tell him you don't think things will work out between the two of you, and you're really too busy to go out. End of story. Period." Having never had to use such a line, I was amazed at the ease with which it poured forth.

Now it was her turn to laugh. "I suppose you're right. He's not the kind to stalk me or something."

I wished she hadn't said that. The word "stalking" brought my fears back up to the surface.

Claire apparently didn't pick up on my anxiety. "So, how's the pregnancy, and Sunday night aside, how is everyone taking the news?"

I fiddled with my silverware, wishing the moussaka we'd both ordered would arrive. "Mike's overjoyed," I began tentatively, "and I think Em is too. Maggie is less enthusiastic—you know, embarrassed that we would let this happen. Keisha, for reasons of her own, is ecstatic, because it will mean more responsibility for her. I think I'll send her to get her real estate license. I can still be the broker."

Claire pondered for a minute. "Let's go back to Maggie. She's at the age, sweetie. You're her mother and everything you do is bound to displease her...."

Now there was a comforting thought.

"What is it psychologists say? She's trying hard to separate herself from you, to become a person in her own right. Be grateful she hasn't gone in for piercings or tattoos."

"Mike would kill her," I muttered.

The moussaka arrived, and we both ate as if we hadn't eaten all day. Conversation stopped, and afterward, as we lingered over the last of her second glass of wine, our talk turned to happier things and a bit of gossip. Like Keisha and José. I kept my lip buttoned, since poor José didn't know he was getting married, at least as far as I knew. Finally I glanced at my watch.

"Omigosh, it's nine-thirty. Mike and the girls will be pacing the floor. We've got to go." So we paid the bill, and I drove Claire home, promising we'd have another girls' night soon. In spite of the heavy nature of some of the talk, the evening had bolstered my spirits. As I drove home, I vowed to get serious with Keisha about this wedding she was planning. I'd heard of grooms surprising their brides with instant weddings, but never the other way around. Leave it to Keisha to break tradition.

Chapter Five

I pulled my car up next to Mike's in the enlarged parking space we'd made by the guesthouse. Daylight saving had ended, and it was pitch dark, so I decided to walk around to the front door because somehow the back yard lights were out, and the front porch was well lit. I knew my way down the driveway well enough to make it in the dark.

I started down the driveway and saw out of the corner of my eye movement in the bushes to the side. Just as I screamed, a dark figure ran toward me and before I could move head-butted me in the stomach—so hard that I lost my breath and fell on my back on the driveway. Within seconds Mike and the girls were outside, Gus having heard my scream if they didn't. The figure was gone. Mike paused only a second to make sure I was breathing and talking and then took off to find the assailant, calling over his shoulder for Maggie to stay with me and Em to go call 911.

I lay still until I felt my breath come back, and then I struggled to a sitting position. Ever so gently, Maggie pushed me back down. "Stay there until Mike comes," she said. Fourteen-year-olds can be so bossy!

Em rejoined us, holding my hand and repeating, "They said they'd be right here." Then she looked nervously down the driveway and asked, "Where's Mike? We need him." Em and her comforting belief that Mike could save any situation!

The police arrived before Mike, though he came running up, winded, right after that. Bending over to catch his breath, he said, "I saw a car drive away about a block and a half north, but I have no proof it was whoever attacked Kelly." Finally he turned his attention to me. "Where does it hurt?"

"Nowhere. Well, my belly's sore where he hit me, and I think my back is roughed up from landing on the driveway. My head's okay— I really landed on my butt and then sort of drifted the rest of the way down."

Mike turned to one of the officers. "Call an ambulance. She's got a baby in that belly."

"Mike, I am not going to the hospital."

"You are going to lie right there until the EMTs check you and I can call Dr. Goodwin."

I mentally retreated but managed to murmur, "Don't tell Mom." Cynthia O'Connell would have been here in a flash, fussing over me until I got up and ran off into the darkness out of desperation.

"I won't, if you promise to lie still. I don't want to lose our baby."

It wasn't me he was worried about—it was the baby! *Not a fair thought, Kelly.*

I lay still. And I worried. I worried about bleeding, a sign I might lose the baby. Did my pants feel damp? Was it just evening dampness and lying on the ground? This baby had been a surprise, one that caught me off guard, but now the thought I might lose it sent me into a panic. I couldn't, but yes…I'd worked myself into such a state I was having a hard time breathing. The girls stayed by me, and I could hear Maggie saying, "Take deep slow breaths, Mom."

José appeared on my other side and grasped my hand. "You're gonna be okay, Miss Kelly. Keisha will kill me if I let anything happen to you."

I tried to smile but it didn't really work. "José," I said, panting to talk, "please call her. We need her over here right now."

"Will do." He stood and punched the buttons on his phone.

The EMTs brushed the girls out of the way, though I held out a hand to them. "We're right here, Mom." It was Em's quavering voice.

The EMTs poked, listened to my heart, asked the same questions over and over, and then asked who my obstetrician was—Mike must have told them about the baby. Then I was loaded, oh so carefully, onto a gurney and rolled to the ambulance.

"I'm not going to the hospital! I'm okay. I'll be fine if I can just sleep in my own bed."

Mike was right there. "Kelly, stop. They need to check you in private. If you need to go to the hospital, you will."

Mike rode in the ambulance with me, clutching my hand, stroking my forehead, pushing my hair, now damp with perspiration and evening air, off my face.

"The girls!" I struggled to sit up.

"José is with them, and Keisha's on her way. They're fine but worried about you."

I started to cry. "Mike, this is so scary for them. Let's just go back home so they won't be frightened." I struggled to sit up again, but his arms held me down.

"No, Kelly. They'd be more frightened if they thought you weren't getting the medical attention you need."

For once, we didn't go to the county hospital. Sherrie Goodwin had privileges at a downtown hospital, where I admit the accommodations were a bit nicer. But an ER is an ER, and I was undressed, gowned, and subjected to more questions.

Just my luck, there was a female EMT, and she checked my underwear. In a soothing, reassuring voice, she said, "Just a few little red spots. No serious bleeding. But we've talked to your doctor, and she wants you in the hospital overnight for observation."

Red spots! Blood! Oh, God, please don't let me lose this baby. My mind had wandered far from the subject of who hit me and why. The paramedic gave me a shot, and pretty soon I didn't care…didn't care if I was going to the hospital, didn't care if I didn't know who did this or why, but even in my foggy state, I clung to the prayer for my baby.

I would stay overnight for observation. Mike made it clear that was Dr. Goodwin's order and she would be in next morning to check on me. He also made it clear I was not to object.

"The girls?"

"Keisha's with them. I'm spending the night here on that…uh…cot." He looked distastefully at the cot on the wall opposite my bed. "Wish I could climb in with you."

"Mike!" I pretended shock.

"Don't misinterpret. It just looks a lot more comfortable, and I could hold you."

I smiled, and he leaned down for a big kiss. "Tomorrow night," I said.

Predictably, nurses came in every two hours to take my blood pressure and temperature and check my nether regions. "No more spotting, Ms. O'Connell. I think you and that tiny baby are going to be fine." I breathed a sigh of relief.

Of course, it's hard to sleep in two-hour segments, and neither of us slept well. Inevitably, when the nurse departed, with her cheery bit of good news, I wanted to go back to sleep. Mike wanted to talk about who did this and why.

"Kelly, you must have seen something. Describe the man for me."

I sighed. I'd been over this so many times. "I think it was a man but I'm not even sure about that. If it was, he was slight, not tall, not heavy. He packed a wallop with his head though." I rubbed my sore belly.

"I've thought about all your adventures, Kelly…."

I started to protest, but he raised a hand. "No other word for it. Ralphie who killed those old women and almost killed your mother and you is safely locked away in a mental institution; John Henry with his big box store that was a front for drugs is locked away; that Wilson character who was dealing drugs is dead. And the Reverend Dr. Bruce Hollister is also locked away."

"So is Jo Ellen North," I said. "Why'd you leave her out?"

"Because my mind keeps coming back to her. Of all the people you've tangled with, she was the most vengeful, the most…oh, what's the word I want? …sociopathic I suppose. And she has more reason for revenge now."

"Mike, she's in prison. Her parents are dead. And she had no siblings. It's not like she's pulling strings from inside the penitentiary."

He hung his head and stared at his hands. "That's what I keep worrying about. What don't we know? I'm calling the warden tomorrow."

"Fine," I yawned. "You do that. My baby and I want to go to

sleep."

"Kelly!" It was a whispered protest, but I noticed he fell asleep before I did.

Next morning I was tired, stiff, sore, and grumpy. When a resident came in and said I was fine and about to be dismissed, I almost argued with him.

"Dr. Goodwin has asked that you go by her office on your way home. She'll fit you in to her schedule."

All I wanted was to go home and crawl in my own bed, preferably without Mike at this point. I slowly got out of bed and stood on legs that were decidedly wobbly. In all the commotion last night, Mike hadn't thought to bring me any fresh clothes, so I put on the pants and blouse I'd been wearing and looked with distaste at the jacket probably permanently scarred with dirt and gravel. The blouse had bits of blood on it, so I finally threw the jacket over my shoulders and climbed back into bed. The whole process exhausted me.

While we were waiting for discharge paperwork, which seemed to take forever, Mike tried to run his district from his cell phone, and I called Keisha. She was by then at the office, having fixed the girls breakfast, packed their lunches, and delivered them to school.

"I missed my breakfast with José," she said with a hint of complaint. But then, with more cheer, "I guess that ain't the most important thing in the world. We got to figure out who's trying to kill you."

It hadn't really occurred to me that someone was trying to kill me—maybe after last night trying to kill my baby. But I thought they were just harassing me, albeit to an extreme degree.

Keisha didn't stop while I thought this through but talked right on. "I'm gettin' on the computer right now and start looking into things. Don't you worry. And I'll get the girls from school and fix supper. You rest."

"We can order something from the Grill," I suggested tentatively.

"Those girls will love my fried chicken and mashed potatoes. I'm fixing supper."

I thanked her and hung up, just as the nurse came bustling in with my discharge papers, followed by an orderly pushing a wheelchair.

"I can walk," I said, climbing out of bed. But my legs threatened to give way again, and Mike caught me just in time.

"Hospital rules," the nurse said crisply.

"Oh, okay," and I sank into the wheelchair, trying to hold my head up and not show how grateful I was to be pushed by someone.

By the time we got to Dr. Goodwin's office, I was feeling a bit better but had this strange feeling of being detached from the world around me.

"Being in the hospital, even briefly, can do that to you," Mike said, patting my knee in what I'm sure he thought was a comforting way but I found sort of patronizing.

He held on to me going from the parking lot to the doctor's office, and my mind flashed back to the day a stalker had shot at me, Ms. Lorna, and her daughter Sheila, with a high-powered rifle as we walked across the same parking lot. Came within a hair of killing Sheila. Now, with Mike, I felt safe.

The receptionist greeted us happily, though I could see curiosity in her eyes. "Ms. Buxton will show you in," she said, and Sally Buxton appeared magically.

"Ms. O'Connell, what did you do? We'll have to see that you take better care of yourself." She took us directly into Dr. Goodwin's office. "Just let me take your blood pressure and temperature…for our records, you know." She patted my shoulder—why was everyone patting me today? When she finished, she said, "Temperature and pulse are fine, but blood pressure is a little high. I'll mention it to Doctor. She'll be right in. You take care of yourself now."

She was followed almost immediately by Dr. Goodwin. Hands on hips, she demanded, "Kelly, what am I going to do with you? First you get shot at in my parking lot, and now you nearly lose your baby to some random violence."

No need to tell her it wasn't random, or at least we didn't think so. "Did I really come close to losing the baby?"

She sighed and sat behind her desk. "There's no way to know for sure. I doubt you damaged it, if that's worrying you. But you're still in your first trimester and you're almost an at-risk patient because of your age, so miscarriage is always a possibility." She paused, fiddled with a pencil, and then looked directly at me. "I didn't need to see you today. Hospital reports all look good, but I wanted to stress the importance of taking care of yourself." She looked down at the chart. "Your blood pressure is high. Let me take it again, now that you've been sitting here a while."

She did and announced, "Perfectly normal. Must have been stress."

I let out a sigh of relief. High blood pressure in pregnancy scared me. It led to eclampsia, though I knew that usually came later in a pregnancy.

Dr. Goodwin continued her lecture. "This is Wednesday. I don't want you to go back to work until Monday. Sleep a lot, work from home if you have to, but stay home."

"Probably be safer not out in public," Mike muttered, but when Dr. Goodwin said, "Pardon me?" he just waved it away with a low, "Nothing. Talking to myself."

She looked puzzled and turned back to me. "How's the morning sickness?"

"Almost gone. Not really a problem."

She asked about fatigue and I almost snapped that I was tired because I barely had any sleep last night, but I admitted that I was tired a lot.

"Then sleep. And call me if you show the least sign of spotting." She stood, indicating the visit was over, and putting an arm around my shoulders, finished with, "I'm counting on you to take care of yourself and that baby."

At least she hadn't told Mike to "take care of the little woman." We thanked her and left.

We got home about two o'clock, and I felt like it was midnight. I immediately headed for a shower, clean clothes and bed. Mike said he had phone calls to make and office work he could do from home. He didn't want to leave me alone.

Sleepy as I was, I turned on him and said, "Mike, you can't stay home with me every day. You'd lose your job. And don't expect me to stay home for the rest of this pregnancy. That might delight Keisha, but I want to work. I need to work for my health as well as the income."

And with that I stalked off upstairs and did not hear his soft, "I'm working on some things."

****

I woke to the house smelling wonderfully of fried chicken, the kind my mom never made from scratch. Throwing on some of my nicer sweats, I wandered downstairs to find Mike helping the girls with their homework—quietly. Maggie was intent on algebra, which Mike was able to help her with and I never was. Em was creating something on her sketchpad, her lips clamped in concentration.

Keisha was in the kitchen mashing potatoes while the chicken warmed in the oven. When I offered to throw together a salad, she told me to sit at the kitchen table and watch. We were having Mike's favorite green beans—with bacon, onion, and vinegar.

And so we gathered at the table for a great, home-cooked meal. Mike and I cooked—me on school nights and he on weekends—but I would never have tried fried chicken. I found myself ravenous but also tickled that the girls ate with such relish.

"Keisha," Mike said, "you don't need to work in a realtor's office. Why don't you move into the guest house and be our cook and nanny?"

"And what would I do with José?" she asked archly. "I want us to have our own house."

That launched a discussion of wedding plans, and I asked bluntly if José knew yet that he was getting married.

"He's got some idea," she grinned. "We been talking about it."

The girls, who had no idea about this, were open-mouthed. Once the idea sank in, Em jumped up and asked, "Am I too old to be a flower girl?"

"Maybe you both can be junior bridesmaids," Keisha drawled, "but José won't put up with a big, fancy affair. It's gonna be small, maybe even City Hall. But first we gotta make sure your momma's safe."

Both girls glanced at me, though Maggie turned away quickly, a shadow erasing the smile she'd had.

Mike cleared his throat. "I called the women's prison today. Talked to the warden who checked the records. Jo Ellen North has had no visitors, gets very little mail, makes no phone calls. That doesn't mean some other inmate might not have gotten her a disposable cell phone."

"Jo Ellen North?" Maggie exclaimed. "The lady who tried to kill you when we were little? Is that what this is all about?" She stood up, threw her napkin on the table, and stalked off to her bedroom.

The rest of us stared after her in awed silence. There was no mistaking the slam of her bedroom door. Mike put his napkin on the table and started to rise, saying, "I'll go after her."

"No, let me. This is a mother/daughter thing, and it goes beyond Jo Ellen North."

Behind me I heard Keisha say, "Miss Em, let's you and me clear this table. I got to take some chicken for José."

Maggie had thrown herself face down on her bed and was crying into her pillow—softly, not loud sobs, but nonetheless crying. I sat and stroked her head gently, but she appeared to ignore me. At least she didn't tell me to go away. Finally after a long silence, I asked, "Can you tell me about it? Surely the mention of Jo Ellen North didn't upset you that much. She's safely away in prison and can't hurt us."

She rolled over and propped her head up on one hand. "No, but it never stops, Mom. You promise and promise and some new threat comes along. The kids at school think I lead an exciting life...except Jenny, who knows better."

"Whatever's going on now, I didn't do anything to set it off. I'm not looking into murder, or drug deals, or anything. It may be part of living with a police officer, but you wouldn't get rid of Mike for that reason, would you?"

She shook her head. "No, Mike's cool. I'm glad he's our father now, but no one ever threatens him—it's always you." She paused, bit her lip, and looked away. "And now there's gonna be a new baby. Kind of embarrassing at my age...."

Her age! What did she think about my age? But I managed to hold that comment back.

"And I suppose I'll have to babysit and change diapers and all that stuff."

"Not if you don't want to." I made myself a promise then and there that the girls' lives would not change because of this baby.

She shook her head restlessly. "I don't know. Nothing seems right. I want to be six years old again...or else I want to go to college next year. I hate school, hate the way I look...." She buried her face in the pillow again, but I pulled her upright and hugged her tight and hard. There were all kinds of things I wanted to say about being a teenager and finding herself and the success of late bloomers and all the stuff a mom wants to say to a teenager, but I just held on to her.

When I finally let go and held her at arms' length so I could look at her, she said, "I'll come do dishes in a minute."

"No. Keisha and I will do them. You take some private time. Just remember we all love you, and I will never let anyone hurt you."

"What about you? What happens to Em and me if something happens to you?"

"It won't," I said fiercely.

Maggie didn't come back out that night, but just before I went to sleep, I sneaked into her room and found her sleeping soundly. Once again, I sat stroking her hair, but she didn't stir.

Chapter Six

The next morning, Maggie seemed herself at breakfast, and I was relieved. Mike had an early appointment, so Keisha came to take the girls to school. Maggie gave me a fierce hug and said, 'I love you." I hugged back, but I knew she would never have done that at school. There, she would have hurried away from the car as fast as she could, as though anxious to disavow any knowledge of me.

So I was home, with a whole day before me to rest, relax, piddle and do some work for my lagging business, which was being severely ignored these days. I was carefully locked in with the alarm set. Mike had found the alarm necklace I got when he was home alone after his automobile accident and made me promise to wear it. In addition, he made me promise to keep my gun handy as I went from room to room. *Good gravy! Does he think Isis is after me?*

I spent most of the morning in our shared office, a cup of decaf at my elbow. On my own, without the doctor telling me, I'd cut out caffeine except for an occasional bite of chocolate. I booted the computer and cleaned up a lot of office files, something I should have done long ago—weeding out old referrals that had come to nothing, adding new listings that needed to be checked out, checking MLS listings to keep myself knowledgeable of what was going on in the area and what houses were available. After all, I couldn't just sell the houses I had listed.

Keisha called to give me a couple of messages.

"Kelly, you sure there's not something else suspicious? Some house you sold that had something funky about it? A family in the neighborhood you've rubbed the wrong way?"

I'd have to have rubbed really hard to make them this serious about revenge. I didn't say that to Keisha, and she went on. "Someone whose house didn't sell?"

Finally I broke into the litany of suspects and said, "Keisha, none of the things you've said are worth burning down a guest house or head butting a pregnant woman. Yes, I think whoever did it knows I'm pregnant. What I can't figure is why they went back from burning the guesthouse to the sugar thing. One's vandalism, the other's harassment. They're two totally different things, two totally different levels of trouble."

"I been thinking about that, too, Kelly. Can't figure it. José is no help. He just listens and doesn't talk."

"He's probably thinking about marriage," I said. "I'm gonna fix myself some lunch."

"You want me to get something from the Grill?"

"No, I think I'll scramble some eggs." And that's just what I did. Then I checked all the doors one more time—Mike and Keisha were making me paranoid—and took the latest Deborah Crombie novel up to our bedroom. I read four pages before I fell sound asleep—no reflection on the book.

I slept hard for two hours and woke suddenly. One look at the clock sent me scurrying downstairs—Keisha would be bringing the girls any minute. I unlocked the front door, turned off the alarm system, and set myself to fixing snacks. Today I decided on sliced bananas with a scoop of Nutella on each plate. Healthy and good. My mind turned to supper, and I studied the contents of the freezer without much inspiration. Tuna in the cupboard didn't inspire either, but I pulled out a can of salmon and decided on croquettes. My mom made them when I was a kid, and I loved them. I'd call and ask for directions.

I got so lost in planning my cooking that I lost track of time and realized with a jolt that it was after three-thirty, and Keisha and the girls should have long been here. Just as I puzzled about that, my cell phone rang.

"Kelly? I can't find Maggie anywhere. She's not out front where she usually waits for us, and I sent Em in to the office to ask, but they don't have no idea. Now everybody's in an uproar, and I don't know what to do to find that child."

My heart sank to the bottom of my bare feet. I couldn't decide whether to weep or scream or call Mike. Surprisingly, I answered kind of calmly. "Ask the school to keep a lookout, but bring Em on home. I have an idea where she might be." The phone rang again almost immediately. It was the middle school principal.

"Ms. O'Connell, we've looked everywhere, and we simply can't find Maggie. We're *very* concerned. After all, we're responsible for our children's safety while they're on the grounds. Of course, Maggie wasn't really on the grounds…or in our care since school's out for the day."

In my panic, I paused long enough to wonder if Mr. Stanush was building the school's defense in case Maggie really disappeared and we sued. I could hear Mike telling me not to jump to the worst scenario.

Without stopping for makeup or to change out of my sweats, I thrust my feet into the handiest shoes—worn tennis shoes. Maggie would be embarrassed by my appearance. At least I finger-combed my hair, which was probably still wild on one side of my head and squished on the right side that I slept on. I was out the driveway before Keisha and Em returned, and I knew exactly where I was going.

Bun Appetit was experiencing an afternoon lull when I stormed in. Mona looked up from the counter where she sat working on some papers and pointed wordlessly to the kitchen. Maggie and Jenny sat on stools, eating the small ice cream cups Mona kept for kids' treats.

Something held me back. I didn't storm. I walked in calmly and said, "Maggie, Keisha and I were worried about you."

She didn't really look surprised to see me, but she hung her head. "Sorry, Mom. I just…I wasn't ready to go home. Jenny let me come here, and she listened to me…."

Dear God, I wanted to scream, *do I not listen to you?* And then it occurred to me that I really didn't listen to her. Even in the talk we'd had the night before, I'd been justifying myself, not really listening to Maggie.

Jenny had faded away, going out front with her mom, and I simply held my arms out, and Maggie walked into them. I realized that she was almost as tall as me. I pulled her head onto my shoulder, and finally let go of the sobs I'd been holding back. Maggie was crying too, though more quietly, and I was struck again with how much everything in her world was changing…and how fast.

When I finally mastered my emotions—well, almost—I said, "Maggie, as long as Mona agrees, you can come here any time but you must let me know where you are. Otherwise my imagination runs wild, and I think of all kinds of horrible things. I just need to know you're safe, baby."

She nodded but didn't say anything, and I wondered how deep

the hurt in this child was. Only then did she think to say, "Mom, you've got your sleeping clothes on!" She was predictably horrified.

"That's how frantic I was," I said.

Mona came in softly, and I asked her to call the school and report that Maggie was safe. I'd go up there in the morning to make sure they took no disciplinary action. This wasn't willful disobedience—it was a cry for help.

Mona sent us home with hot dogs for everyone, over my protests that I had supper all planned. "Nonsense. You don't need to cook. You're supposed to be resting. It's the least I can do." She turned to hug Maggie. "Sweetie, you're welcome here any time. In fact, this summer I may put you to work with Jenny. But for now, you keep in touch with your mom."

Maggie brightened at the idea of work and thanked Mona.

When we got home, Em, hands on hips, threatened, "You are in so much trouble, Maggie. Whew! I'm glad it's not me."

"Em! Do your homework and pay attention to yourself and not Maggie's business. Maggie, you better start on your homework."

Keisha was in the kitchen, boiling potatoes, cutting up celery and scallions. She merely raised an eyebrow at me. I dumped the hot dog sack on the table and asked, "What are you doing?"

"Making potato salad to go along with those hot dogs you got there," she said complacently, turning back to slicing the scallions.

"How did...." I stopped myself. I didn't want to hear about sixth sense again.

"No sixth sense, Kelly. Logic. Maggie would go to Jenny, and Mona wouldn't let you come home without supper. Sixth sense ain't always the answer."

I shut up and poured myself a glass of water and decided I liked a lot better than sparkling cider. But I'll admit to a longing for chardonnay. I rubbed my belly to remind myself why I wasn't drinking wine.

"Mom?" Maggie appeared in the kitchen, her voice tentative. "Are you going to tell Mike about today?"

I thought a minute. "No, I'm not. You are."

When she went back to the dining table and her homework, Keisha uncharacteristically began to preach. "You know, Kelly, not all girls have people like Jenny and Mona to go to. They end up wandering the streets…it ain't pretty."

A part of me wondered how much of that Keisha knew from personal experience, but I simply said, "I know I'm lucky. I also know she's a much better kid than most runaways. I don't want to think about what could have been."

When Mike came home, he kissed me, greeted Keisha and the girls, and headed upstairs to change clothes. As he headed toward the bedroom wing, Maggie said, "Mike? Get you a beer?"

He looked startled, then saw me nod ever so slightly, and said, "Sure, Mag. I'll be right down."

When he came downstairs, she took him by the hand and led him to her bedroom. I heard the door close softly behind them.

It was a long fifteen minutes before Mike came out, and when he did his face told me nothing. "Mag's finishing her homework in her room," was his noncommittal comment. Keisha refused to stay for dinner, sensing we needed to be a family that night, so I sent a hot dog and some potato salad with her.

After dinner, I finished in the kitchen and sat down with the

Crombie novel I'd fallen asleep over that afternoon. Mike was reading a book on Fort Worth history—his favorite subject—and Em was busy at some project, not homework I deduced but something she'd thought up to do. About eight I reminded her it was time to think about bath and bed, and by eight-thirty I got pretty determined about it. I'd already heard the shower running so I knew Maggie was through with the bathroom.

Finally, the girls were asleep, and we trudged up to our room. *How can I be so tired when I haven't done anything all day?* But I was exhausted.

"Are you going to tell me about your talk with Maggie?"

He shook his head. "It's between Maggie and me. I will tell you she loves you a lot, but right now she's feeling smothered, angry, confused....all those things teenage girls feel."

"And boys don't?" My tone was sarcastic.

"Oh, yeah, they do. But it's not the same. If Snickerdoodle is a boy, he and I are bound to have some pretty big rows."

That seemed to end the discussion, and I climbed into bed. Mike picked up the biography of John Quincy Adams that he kept on the bedside table. He was working his way slowly through it, at the rate of a few pages a night. The girls would be in college before he finished it.

****

I did as Sherrie Goodwin ordered and stayed home. I read, worked, and napped and finally got to the point I didn't feel guilty about any of it. I learned a few things during those days: nothing catastrophic happened at the office, and Keisha even made headway with a few properties I'd been working on. She roughed out bids on the places we'd decided on for rental purchases. And I found I could work effectively from home. I could feel the balance of my life changing, and maybe it was the euphoria of early pregnancy, but I wasn't all that unhappy about it. I decided to ease into my new life by spending one day a week at home. After all, I had a new baby to plan for.

Friday and Saturday night we went out for supper—once to the Grill and once to the Middle Eastern restaurant we all liked. Sunday Mike put a roast in the oven with potatoes nestled around it and declared we'd have good sandwiches for a few days. Monday I went back to work.

Keisha was businesslike. "Mornin'. You have a chance to look at those contract offers?"

"May I have a cup of coffee first? I'll get it." When I was settled at my desk, I said, "Yes, I looked. They're good. I think as an initial offer you could go lower on both places, but not a lot."

"You don't want to scare them off," she said a bit defensively.

"No, but you don't want to overpay for the properties either, especially the one Anthony is going to have to redo."

Anthony had gone by and looked carefully at the re-do. He pronounced it salvageable, even said it had good bones. But he added, "Mother of God, it suffers from deferred maintenance." A phrase he'd learned from me.

We got that settled, and Keisha asked about Maggie. "I didn't want to bother you all this weekend, and José kept me pretty busy"—said with a slight grin—"but how's my Maggie girl?"

"Hard to tell. She spends a lot of time in her room with the door shut, and I know she's on the phone a lot, both texting and talking. Mike had to take her to task for her minutes the other day."

"Mike?"

"Uh, yeah. He's sort of taken over some of the communication with Maggie on things that might look to her like discipline coming from me. That part's sort of hard on me, but it's working. And she's pleasant when she's not in her room—aside from squabbles with her sister."

"She'll be all right. Okay, what about the stalker?"

"No sign. Nothing."

"He ain't through," she said as though she'd just talked with whoever it was and knew this for a certainty. "I've been making a list. We can't rule anybody out, including Jo Ellen North."

I didn't have the heart to tell her that Mike and I had already ruled out most of the possibilities from my past adventures.

"The only one we can cross off the list is Ralphie," she said.

Ralph Conaster was a peculiar fellow with a strange grudge against older women from his mother's church circle. He snapped and starting killing them. All of Fairmount was in a panic about a serial killer just when my mom moved here. But I didn't know it was Ralph or Ralphie as we came to call him, when he started to court Mom. That escapade nearly cost Mom and me our lives, but Ralphie was now safely confined in an institution.

"He didn't have any friends or relatives to be angry with you," Keisha went on. "But now John Henry—he had cohorts and unsavory connections, including pot dealers. Might be one of them is angry at their big deal gone wrong. Or John Henry could have bribed someone in prison who just now got out and came after you."

John Henry Jackson wanted to build a big-box grocery in our historic neighborhood, and I organized a neighborhood battle to preserve the historic character of Magnolia Avenue. Only John Henry intended to use his "farm fresh" store as a front for growing and selling marijuana. When his scheme came out, he tried—and nearly succeeded—to take me to Mexico on a one-way trip. But I doubted John Henry's reach extended from prison.

"Sheila said she doesn't think any of Bruce Hollister's former church members would be that anxious to get revenge for him. In fact the church fell apart soon after he went to prison for kidnapping her. And that hit man he hired—he's long out of the country."

"So," Keisha said, "that still leaves Jo Ellen North. You sure she didn't have siblings? A cousin maybe? One of her father's business associates? Someone besides Jo Ellen who's mad that you're getting a bundle of money?"

I shook my head. "Mike checked with the warden. Jo Ellen doesn't get letters or phone calls, no visitors. I guess her husband divorced her, probably happy for a reason."

"Well, somebody's giving the orders here. Somebody didn't just come out of the woodwork and start harrassing you. I still think the answer is somewhere in your life the last few years."

"Did you ever think someone might be after Mike?"

"Nope." She turned back to her computer.

I was tired of talking about the stalker. Perhaps it was denial, but deep down the fact was the stalker had really scared me. I knew, like Keisha, that he wasn't gone. He was playing a waiting game, and it did just what he wanted—it made me nervous.

"Let's talk about your wedding," I said brightly.

"How'd you know José proposed?" she demanded.

Chapter Seven

My subterfuge worked, and I was able to distract Keisha from the stalker to weddings. "When did he propose?" I asked.

She looked almost coy. "Well, I had to tell him it was time. But then he did just what his momma told him. First—and I didn't know about this—he went to my momma's house and asked for her blessing. 'Course she likes José but she wouldn't have said anything if she didn't. She knows she can't stop me when I'm determined…and I am determined about this. So then José went and got a ring"—she flashed it in the air and then said sheepishly, "It's zircon but he's saving for a real one, and I get to pick it out."

"I hope you'll be modest in your choice," I said as tactfully as I could. Keisha was given to the flamboyant, and I didn't want to see them in hock for the next ten years for a ring.

Her expression was odd, a little bit defensive. "'Course I will. I got plans for us, and a house is more important than a ring. But anyway, he took me to Lili's and they had a bouquet on the table and everything. All the wait staff was in on it, and they was grinning. José started to get down on one knee, but I told him he was blocking traffic and he better sit down in his seat."

By this time, tears of laughter were rolling down my cheeks. "So he proposed?"

"Naw, he didn't actually say anything. He just pulled out this ring, and I put my finger out, and he put it on. Then everyone cheered, and we got a bottle of champagne on the house. I don't think it was the best they had, but it was pretty good."

My mind was reeling with pictures of the surprised patrons in the restaurant that night. "And?" I asked.

"And nothing. We had dinner—steak for him and scallops for me—and then we went home. And here I am today like nothin's changed. But it has. I'm moving ahead with my life plan."

I knew her life plan included a real estate license, and it was on my mind, but I put it aside for a bit. "When's the wedding? Still City Hall?"

She stalled. Got herself another cup of coffee and waved the pot toward me, but one cup was almost too much for me these days. Then she paced, while I watched, my lips twitching as I hid a smile.

Finally. "You think Peter would let me have it in the back room of the Grill?"

I was flabbergasted. "What night?"

"I don't know. They're closed Sundays, and I know they can't turn their regular weekend customers away. Maybe a Tuesday night?"

Tuesday seemed an odd day for a wedding, but it wasn't mine so I said, "All you can do is ask him."

The usually bold Keisha turned timid. "Would you…we could have lunch there…my treat."

I smiled at the chink in her usual bravado. "Of course, meantime, let's get some work done. What have you found out about real estate classes?"

She was suddenly all business. "I'm confused," she admitted.

"There's online courses, and a private institute, and a course from the state university in Arlington. That sounds best to me but it's expensive. I can't afford that, Kelly. Not and marry José too."

I wasn't about to force her to make that choice. "Why don't you investigate scholarships and loans from UTA and then we'll talk about it. The beauty of an online course is you could do it and keep things running here in the office when I'm out." My first venture toward the subject of a four-day workweek for me.

She just looked at me and then turned to her computer, where I could tell she was rapidly checking scholarships. All you ever had to do with Keisha was throw her a challenge.

We went to lunch at the Grill early to beat the crowd. Settled in a booth with our turkey burgers, I began to munch but I noticed Keisha looking around nervously.

"Why don't you just ask Peter to stop by when he has time?

She looked at me. "What? You got the sixth sense too?"

"I can tell you're nervous about asking him. Best get it over with."

Peter, so charming, so willing to help, came over almost as soon as she talked to him. When she suggested her plan, he said, "You ladies mind if I sit down for a minute?"

Peter never sat with customers, which he considered an intrusion into his diners' time. Obviously he was breaking precedent which meant this floored him.

Finally, he echoed, "A wedding?" and took a handkerchief from his pocket to wipe his forehead. "Do I get to give the bride away?"

I swear Keisha blushed, though it was hard to tell with her complexion. "Maybe so," she said. "I hadn't thought that far."

She thought of everything else, why not this?

Peter smiled. "Just joking. Maybe Mike should give you away. I'll throw rose petals or whatever."

"No rice. It's not safe," she said.

Peter agreed. "I hear it can explode in birds' stomachs."

Keisha favored him with a disdainful look. "Nope, but it makes floors slippery and people can fall. And it would be an unholy mess to clean up."

That sort of silenced the discussion, and Peter finally said, "Let me think about this. When you have more specific details, come see me. Like what time, exactly what date, what food you want to serve."

Keisha nodded and thanked him, but her mind had obviously already moved on.

"I think almost thirty people, don't you, Kelly? All the people at our Sunday dinners, plus my momma and José's folks."

José's real name is Joe Thornberry. His mom's Hispanic, and his dad Anglo, I guess. But when Keisha dragged him into our family circle, we already had a Joe—who was full Hispanic and was Theresa's husband. Keisha unofficially re-christened her Joe as José; he never complained, and it stuck. These days almost everyone but his folks called him José.

"Your sister," I suggested.

"Nah, she'd just bring that baby what cries all the time."

We finished our lunch without deciding on much more detail. Keisha wanted to have it well before my baby arrived so that made us look at late March or early April. But I stressed that José had to be consulted, and she promised. She went off to look again at the Craftsman and talk terms with the owners—I was letting her handle this since it was a rental and didn't really require a license, yet it was good experience for her. I found myself anxious for her to get a license.

Just before I left the office to get the girls, the phone rang and a woman's voice said, "I'm interested in the house you have for sale on Washington."

"I'll be glad to help you. Would you like to see it?" All the while I was wondering why she was interested. It was smallish, unpretentious house in need of redoing but not interesting enough for me to put Anthony on the project.

"I thought I'd send my assistant. His name's Sanford. Would nine in the morning suit?"

This was growing stranger by the minute. If she could afford an assistant, why was she interested in this property? Rental? Even I had discarded that idea. "Nine-fifteen would be better. I have to get my girls to school."

"Of course. Thank you."

Quickly before she hung up, I asked, "Could I have your name and a phone number? I'm sure your assistant will report back, but I'd like to be able to call."

"That won't be necessary. I'll contact you after he's reported to me. Thank you for your help."

A decisive silence told me she'd clicked off. I looked at caller ID and scribbled down a number that was clearly for a cell phone. Something about this call disturbed me—in fact, several somethings. Whoever this woman was, she didn't know much about the way to do business or else she was deliberately steamrolling me. Something about her voice—tone, inflection?—sounded familiar and yet I couldn't place it. It was fuzzy, almost distorted…and it dawned on me you can buy devices that disguise your voice. Why would she bother? And her assistant? If he was handling things, why didn't he call? Puzzling all this over, I went to get the girls. Keisha had still not returned.

That afternoon the girls were working diligently at their homework, and I was sitting with them, my thoughts a mile away.

"Mom!" Maggie's tone was impatient to say the least. "I've asked you this three times. Who was the first member of the Catholic Church to run for president?"

My mind struggled both to come back to reality and to come up with the right answer. Finally, I grasped it. "Al Smith. Late 1920s. He was defeated."

She gave me another disgusted look. "I know that."

"Why didn't you just google it?"

"Because you're sitting right here, and I knew you'd know the answer."

Mixed feelings. I was flattered she thought I'd know the answer, but then again I couldn't be doing her homework for her. "Is it in your American history book?"

"We don't have a book. We have a syllabus, and we're supposed to use the internet."

I bit my tongue to keep from saying, "So why didn't you?" Education was changing too much for me.

In truth, I'd been thinking about my strange appointment in the morning. I'd left an explicit note for Keisha telling her what time, what house, but I was still wondering about telling Mike. I knew his answer. He'd forbid me to go. Flat. Period. No argument.

Except there were several things wrong with that. I couldn't run a business if my husband could tell me when and what I could and could not do. Nor was I agreeable to that kind of relationship. And I was so tired of people treating me like an endangered species. Part of it was the pregnancy, but shoot! I'd been pregnant twice before, survived nicely, and produced two pretty fine products. No reason this should be any different.

The big thing, though, was most pregnant women, in their so-called delicate situation, weren't being stalked by a person with unknown intentions. So far, except for the fire, whoever it was couldn't be charged with anything serious—maybe misdemeanor mischief for the sugar in the gas tank episode, and criminal assault for the attack in the driveway. But the incidents were all so different. They didn't fit a pattern…and now this house inspection didn't fit into the pattern that wasn't there. I wasn't convinced that the same person was behind the things that had happened or that he or she had anything to do with tomorrow's appointment. But then another side of my brain admitted that something was off about this appointment. A big something.

I decided not to tell Mike. I was a capable career woman, I'd taken care of myself in some other scary situations, and I intended to do just that in this one. Silently, I promised Mike I'd take my gun and keep it handy. If it turned out to be just what my anonymous caller had said— a woman with an assistant who managed rental property—no big deal. If it turned out to be anything more—well, that was a major problem, but I'd face it when I had to. Only I knew it would be a lot harder to tell Mike afterward and he'd want—no, demand—to know why I didn't tell him before.

"Mom!" Em's voice this time.

"I'm through with my homework. Will you check it?"

I turned to fifth-grade math, which baffled me almost as much as the problem of who was out there with a grudge against me.

I guess I hid my tension well because Mike never once asked what was bothering me, and we had an ordinary evening at home, reading, talking, and—oh, my—making love. After that, I thought I could face a bear the next morning.

Chapter Eight

I've faced situations that put a tight knot in my stomach hours before, but I was quite calm when I dropped the girls off. They, too, were oblivious to any tension, which I told myself was a good sign. I wasn't tense or all of my family would have noticed.

My client—or rather her assistant—kept me waiting fifteen minutes, time I spent rocking in a wooden swing on the porch, which like the rest of the house needed fresh paint. I opened the house—doors and windows—even on this chilly day, hoping the fresh air would blow some of the mustiness out of the house that had been unoccupied for several months. Then I pulled my jacket tightly around me and sat on that swing answering emails.

Charles Sanford, when he appeared, was a slight, young, blond man with polish on his fingernails and a chip on his shoulder. His apologies for being late were perfunctory so I skipped the pleasantries and said brusquely, "Shall we explore the inside?"

He barged through the door, furthering my initial impression of him. As we proceeded from room to room in the three-bedroom, one-bath house, he made derogatory comments such as "Needs a lot of work, doesn't it?" to which I replied, "That's why it's priced the way it is. If your boss wants to buy and rent it, she'll have to put some money in it."

"Why don't you do that yourself?" A question I thought

impertinent and to which I only replied that it didn't fit into my plans.

"I know you're interested in starting a rental business. So I'm curious why not this property?"

I could hardly say I didn't think it was worth fixing and should be a teardown, so I simply said again it didn't fit into my plans right now.

Of the one bath, he said, "Who builds a three-bedroom house with one bathroom?"

"People a century ago," I replied.

As we proceeded through the house, I noticed instead of barging ahead of me, he now kept trying to get behind me. I fingered the gun in my jacket pocket and found it comforting. So far, I'd been able to keep him in sight, but I was disconcerted by the way he watched me. When I pointed out various features—a built-in kitchen cabinet with leaded glass doors, for instance—he muttered, "Nice," but never took his eyes off me.

When he began to ask details of my business that I thought were too personal, I backed off and simply answered by pointing out new features, even places that needed work. A bedroom ceiling that showed a leak, a rotten floorboard. *Good going, Kelly! Who sells a house by showing its flaws?*

I was discussing the plumbing, which thankfully seemed to be in pretty good shape, while he stood against the sink, arms crossed in a belligerent manner. I turned from gesturing to the gas stove—old, but a plus in any house—and noticed his stance.

"Ms. O'Connell, I'm not interested in this house. I'm interested in you." His hand reached, none too subtly, into the inside breast pocket of his jacket.

I'd like to tell you he had the steely blue eyes of a killer, but he didn't. His eyes were brown and at this moment looked a little uncertain. I was not at all uncertain. With one swift gesture I pulled out my handgun, aimed it at him, and said, "I know how to use this."

He was startled, and his protestations of, "Wait a minute! You misunderstand," fell apart when a wicked-looking knife clattered to the floor. He took one look, glanced at me holding the gun steady on him, and bolted out the front door. By the time I followed, he was down the steps and in his car, racing off. I got the last three numbers of his license plate, for what good that would do.

I called Mike. Law officer's wife's privilege—anyone else would call 911. Mike was my 911. To my relief, neither my hands nor my voice were shaking, and I was able to tell him quite calmly what happened.

His terse reply was, "We'll be right there."

A squad car, obviously out on patrol in the neighborhood, beat Mike to the house but not by much. As the young officer began, "Now, Ms. O'Connell, can you tell me what happened?" Mike jumped up the steps to that swing where I once again sat.

"I'll take over," he said too harshly to the officer. "Why didn't you tell me you were showing a house alone today?"

In front of the officer was not the time to ask sarcastically, "Why? Would you have come with me?" A district chief can hardly accompany his wife on her business rounds. I repeated my story that it didn't sound like anything out of the ordinary—a woman who said she managed several properties wanted to send her assistant to look at this property.

He looked around and asked "This house?" Clearly he thought it wasn't worth looking at. "You should have known." It was an outright accusation.

The young officer had walked back down to his car, not quite dismissed but neither sure he was needed. He stood staring out at the street—his attempt, I'm sure, to be discreet.

So I spoke my mind. "Mike, you can't make business decisions for me. Neither can you protect me every minute. You have a job. I have a job. And I think I did pretty well today both doing my job and protecting myself."

I could see his jaw clench and tighten. "Tell me every detail of what happened."

Just as I stated to describe the young man, the knife and all that, my cell rang. I glanced and said, "Keisha." Then I pushed the button and said, "Hello."

"You all right? I got that terrible feelin' again. Should have gone with you."

"I'm fine. Mike's here. I'll tell you about it when I get back to the office."

"Keisha?" Mike asked. "Did she know you were in danger?"

I nodded, and he said, "I wish you had her sixth sense. Okay, go on."

I told him everything, described the young man, told him about my eerie feeling that he was less interested in the house than me, ending with his admission that was true and my pulling my gun, the knife clattering to the floor. "I even got the last three numbers of his license plate, for what good that will do."

"It will help. What kind of car?"

"Silver. Lexus I think. Nice car. Smooth and fast, from the way he took off when he left."

Mike called to the officer, who promptly trotted back up the steps. "Should be a knife in the kitchen on the floor. Bag it, with gloves. Then run a license plate with these last three numbers. Silver Lexus. Fairly new. See if you can get anything."

"Yessir," and the man, a boy really, trotted down the stairs to get an evidence collection kit.

"Kelly, describe this man to me again, carefully, slowly, every detail."

I launched into young, maybe twenty, blond hair, probably not natural, slight build, well dressed, not quite sure of himself. Brown eyes. What else could I think of? I stopped, stymied. No accent but good grammar. Probably good manners. Not a slum kid.

Mike interrupted me. "Kelly, I want you to look at some mug shots with me. You want to meet me at the office?"

I nodded. "Just give me a minute to call Keisha."

"I'll wait."

I wanted to grit my teeth and say, "You can go on. I'll be perfectly fine by myself." But I kept quiet.

He went inside to talk to the officer who was collecting evidence. I had mentioned that the young man had leaned against the sink, perhaps put his hands on the counter, so I suppose they were dusting that for prints too.

Keisha just muttered, "Darn. We're in the thick of it again, Kelly. What have you done this time?"

"Nothing," I said indignantly. "I'll see you later."

Mike and I finally ended up, separately, at the district police headquarters, where he showed me into his office and left saying he'd be back shortly after he collected the mug shots. It took him forever, and I later found out he was compiling a collection of shots of similar looking men. Trying to trick me, I thought.

When he finally came back, he reported that the Lexus had been stolen and was found abandoned on the far west side of Fort Worth. Not a lot of help, but I somehow felt vindicated.

"Now, Kelly," he said, "study each one of these pictures closely. If any look at all like the man this morning, tell me and I'll pull that one out. Then we go again through the ones you've marked." He talked as though I were a not-quite-bright child.

I dutifully studied pictures—a couple sort of looked familiar and I pointed to them. Mike put them aside, and I kept going, until I saw the picture of the man I knew as Charles Sanford. In the picture he had long brown hair, but it was definitely him. Anyone could bleach and cut their hair. "That's him," I said. "No question about it. I don't need to look at any more. I'm sure." There was no name on the picture, just a number. Not that I'd expected it to say Charles Sanford.

Mike had the strangest look on his face that I'd ever seen. "You're absolutely sure?"

I nodded.

"Kelly," he reached for my hand, "that's the kid who beat his girlfriend the night the guest apartment burned. I thought your description sounded like him, but I wanted to make sure. You don't have any doubt?"

"No. But I don't get it—if he was beating his girlfriend, he didn't burn our guesthouse. What's the connection? I don't see any way the two fit together, and yet they must somehow."'

Mike ran a distracted hand over his burr haircut. "I don't know. I can't figure it out either, but I will."

"Mike, that night, he surely didn't use the name Charles Sanford, did he?" Nobody, I thought, would be that dumb.

A look of disgust crossed Mike's face. "Of course not, Kelly. I'd have caught on right away. His name is Greg Davis."

Made sense to me that Charles Sanford was a fake ID, but it was the name he would forever be branded with in my mind. "Did you verify it?"

"The usual things—driver's license, insurance papers, social security card. No, I didn't ask for his birth certificate." Disgust had turned into sarcasm now. "We'll be going back to visit him. Kelly, let me do my job."

I bit my lip and avoided looking at him, which he evidently thought was license to continue his lecture.

"I want you to take Keisha with you on any showings from now on."

We'd been through this before, and it hadn't worked very well. I didn't need or want a chaperone, caretaker, whatever you'd call her. "Mike, I showed this morning I can defend myself, and I'm the one with a license to carry, not Keisha."

"She's working on it," he said, and I knew they'd been in collusion. "She'll have a license pretty quick."

I was a bit put off to be out of the loop—they were, I knew, conspiring to look after me, as though I weren't quite capable myself. Pregnancy, I wanted to shout, does not addle the brain! Instead, calmly as I could, I asked, "Where was the car stolen?"

"River Crest area," he said.

"Where Jo Ellen's father lived. The man who just left me a generous bequest."

"No logical connection, Kelly. This wasn't from his property—which by the way isn't sold because the estate hasn't been 'satisfactorily' settled. We checked. But the car came from the other side of the golf course."

"Still," I persisted, "someone familiar with the area."

"Yeah, and an area where foolish people feel safe leaving their keys in their car. That's what happened. It was stolen sometime last night, out of the owners' unlocked garage."

"There's some connection," I said, "something we have to figure out."

"Kelly," his tone was as patient as he could make it, "some connection the police have to figure out. There's no part of you in the 'we'."

"Am I free to go?" I asked frostily.

He rose and came toward me. "Of course. And sweetheart, don't be mad at me. I'm doing my best to solve a crime and urge you to keep yourself safe. Go have lunch with Keisha and tell her to hurry with that license."

I still left feeling like a kid who'd been scolded instead of a woman who'd done a good job of protecting herself and contributing clues to a possible crime…or a crime to be committed…or I didn't know what.

I marched into my office and announced, "Lunch downtown. My treat. Order filet if you want it."

As Keisha gathered her bag and slipped on her outrageous high heels, she said, "My, my. Are we in a snit?"

"We are," I said firmly.

We had lunch at a new spot where you could overlook the plaza and fountains of Sundance Square. I really longed for a glass of wine as I poured out the story of my morning to Keisha, but I settled for iced tea—knowing I shouldn't even have much of that. "How," I asked, "can this young man be connected to anything else? On the other hand, how can it be coincidence that he's the one who beat his girlfriend?"

"I don't believe in coincidence," Keisha said, "but it sure says something about his character. I don't believe I'd like to have him walking behind me on a dark street. And nobody much scares me."

"You're twice his size," I said and almost giggled.

"But not as sneaky." She stared off in space a moment and then turned to me, her eyes lit with discovery. "Maybe he beat the girl so she'd call 911 and he'd have an alibi when the fire ignited. He could have put grease on the stove on a low flame much earlier."

That was why I liked having Keisha around. One of the reasons.

In spite of a good lunch—Keisha did indeed have a filet, while I settled for a chopped chicken salad—we were no closer to figuring out the puzzle than we had been before. And I was still looking over my shoulder, staring at people on the street, expecting to see Charles Sanford.

****

Back at the office, there was a phone message from the woman whose voice I almost but not quite recognized. Once again her voice sounded distorted. She was terse and to the point. "Charles regrets the misunderstanding. He'd like to set up another appointment."

Not on your life...or mine! I scribbled down the number from caller ID It was a cell phone, and I promptly called Mike with the number. It turned out to be a throwaway cell, which really discouraged me. Charles or whatever his name was didn't really want to reschedule;

his boss lady was just letting me know they were not giving up or being scared away that easily.

I know a bit about the psychology of stalking: rattle the victim so you throw them off base and they make stupid mistakes. One way to do that is the pattern I'd noticed emerging this time—a major event followed by minor things. I was prepared for some minor annoyances in the coming weeks.

Life actually went on fairly peacefully for just about two weeks. Maggie remained generally sullen with occasional bright moods that I tried doubly hard to appreciate when they came. She still spent a lot of time in her room with the door closed. Once I asked Em what Maggie was doing, and she said, "I don't know. She doesn't talk to me anymore." So I wasn't the only one. Maggie was happiest when she played chess with Mike—and beat him. I asked one night if he let her win, and he swore he didn't.

"She a really bright kid. So's Em. Good thing they take after their mother and not their biological father." Then he preened a bit. "'Course I might have had some input as they've been growing up."

I didn't know whether to kick him or hug him. Chose the latter.

My baby bump was beginning to show, morning sickness was behind me, and I was feeling well, if still sleepy. I slept ten hours some nights and still wanted more, and my clothes were getting uncomfortably tight. When Maggie noticed that, she commented,

"Pretty soon the whole world will know our family secret," she said.

"Secret? I didn't know it was a secret. I'm telling people, now that I'm at three months and feel a little safer."

"Why three months?"

So I explained that the danger of miscarriage was great in the first trimester, especially in a woman my age.

She nodded and asked, "You're not going to wear those tight dresses and shirts that cling to your belly, are you?" The implication in her voice was clear.

"No, but I'm going to get some maternity jeans. Wish I'd kept the ones I had when you girls were born."

No comment. She just walked away.

The most troublesome incident with Maggie came one Saturday when she said, a bit too casually, "Oh, Chris is coming over."

"Do I know her?" I asked.

Maggie grinned. "Not her. He's a him. He's a sophomore."

Okay, the moment I'd been awaiting, dreading, wanting to put off until she was thirty. Busying myself straightening the living room, which really didn't need it, I asked, "What's he coming over for?"

"Just to hang out. He's cool. I like him a lot." She sat on the couch, tossing a basketball from one hand to the other. "We'll probably shoot some baskets."

At least she apparently didn't intend to take him to her bedroom and close the door, in which cases I would have had to take dramatic action. Why did Mike go get a haircut when I needed him? Still, it was chilly outside, but maybe shooting baskets would work off some of their heat—take that any way you want. "Shall I invite him to lunch?"

She was aghast. "No, Mom. He'd think you were a dork."

I wasn't sure a dork was the last thing I wanted to be in this case.

"Just keep Em away," Maggie said, and I nodded. Harsh of Maggie, but it only seemed fair.

Chris arrived sometime after ten in the morning. He was, I admit, a bit of a shock. He looked like Charles Sanford/Greg Davis until I convinced myself it was just the longish blond hair with the shock that hung over one eye. He tossed his head frequently to put it back in place. But he had an earring! Granted, just a stud, and just in one ear—but it was an earring. Maggie didn't even have earrings, for Pete's sake.

Maggie's manners were good. "Mom, this is Chris Martin."

His manners were equally good as he held out his hand and said, "Pleased to meetcha."

It was all I could do to keep from replying, "Martin? Uh, has your family lived in Fort Worth for generations?" Maybe he was Robert Martin's grandson. *Stop it, Kelly. Jo Ellen is an only child and she's childless. Besides she wouldn't send a fifteen-year-old boy after me...or would she?*

I managed to reply that I was glad to meet him too.

"We're going out back," Maggie said.

"Okay. Come in when you need a drink."

And they were out the door. Em came through the house and headed for the back door, I put a gentle hand on her shoulder, "Come help me bake cookies."

"Nope. I want to go watch Maggie and her boyfriend."

"That's exactly what you're not going to do. And he's just a friend, not a boyfriend."

She sighed. "He has an earring, you know."

I busied myself with gathering ingredients for the peanut butter cookies I hadn't intended to make.

When Mike came home, he breezed through the kitchen and said, "I think I'll go out back and see if I can outshoot Maggie's friend." He went, slamming the door behind him.

Em gave me a dark look.

****

Claire wanted to host Thanksgiving, but I said I wanted to because Christmas might be too much. We had lunch one day to plan details. Mike and Claire would each roast a turkey, unless Mike wanted to smoke one and roast one fresh. I had nixed his suggestion of frying one. Too dangerous with such a crowd, and I wasn't sure I would like the finished product. We would assign side dishes to everyone.

Claire reported that Megan was going with Brandon to his family's ranch outside Stamford, so that cut our number by two. And Sheila and Don were taking little Lorna to his parents' home in Lamesa. Thanksgiving was looking more manageable.

And then there was Keisha's wedding. Perhaps it would have been proper to call it José and Keisha's wedding, but so far José was a passive participant. After much thought, Keisha chose a Sunday—Peter assured her he would open the restaurant just for her party and would cater his menu to her taste as much as possible. Although it was only mid-November, Keisha and I had several planning sessions at the Grill— where would the altar be? She had a family minister she wanted to perform the ceremony—no, I don't mean someone who has ministered to her family. I meant a distant cousin who was a minister, though of what variety she didn't say. I thought of the Reverend Dr. Bruce Hollister and shivered a bit.

My girls would be her only attendants, and they would wear bright colors—a strong pink for Em and turquoise for Maggie (who would object, I suspected). Mike would be José's best man, to which he had readily agreed, and would walk Keisha down the aisle. No mention was made of giving her away.

Keisha studied and studied the menu at the Grill. Beer and wine for everyone was no problem, but she wanted a seated dinner since there would be maybe forty guests at the most. I hadn't done a head count, but I knew the list had grown. Something light, since it would be warm weather, but not fish—not everyone ate that.

One afternoon in the office, she pounded her desk and said loudly, "That's it!"

Raising my head from some papers, I saw her grinning. "What's it?"

"Hot dogs. Mona will bring that street vendor cart she has and serve hot dogs at the wedding."

I was hesitant to say the least. "Peter may not want you bringing food into his restaurant. And it may even be against the law."

"I'll check, but that's what I want. Peter can provide all the sides and drinks and the wedding cakes—one for me and one for José."

Hot dogs would certainly be economical—and in this case fitting, since we'd helped Mona set up her business—but still she was talking money. "Keisha, have you and José been saving for this day?"

She gave me one of her rolling-eyes looks. "I been savin' for this day since I was ten. Child, I can pay for this wedding and three months' rent on that house."

Silenced, I decided to let her present this idea to Peter without me. Meantime, she hadn't set a date.

Anthony was still working on rebuilding the guesthouse so our property buzzed with subcontractors all day every day—electricians, plumbers, a tile man, and finally painters. I was uncomfortable with strangers on the property and mentioned it to Anthony—who knew if they were Charles Sanford's uncle or neighbor and he'd sent them?

Anthony assured me they were all men he would vouch for. At the office, things were going okay but not great—or maybe between pregnancy and the stalker, I had no heart for it. I had some new listings, a few people looking, and enough to keep us comfortably busy without making me feel crowded, cross, and grumpy.

But all the while, two things worried me. Benjamin Cruze of Bachman and Bannister called one day to say that there had been a delay in getting the will through probate court. An anonymous representative of Robert Martin's family was contesting the bequest to me. No, he couldn't tell me who that was. He or she would disclose the name only to the probate judge. Benjamin promised to keep me apprised of future developments. I thanked him, reassured him I wasn't waiting anxiously for the money, and hung up. But I sat with my hand on the phone, thinking, for a long time. Maybe the stalking wasn't about revenge. Maybe it was about money. And if that was the case, all signs pointed to Jo Ellen North. But how could she manage that from prison?

Mike was discouraged beyond words about the search for Greg Davis/Charles Sanford. "He's simply disappeared from the face of the earth," he said. "No one at the apartment where he lived, no sign of Sandra Balcomb who supposedly lived there. Apartment was empty except for a lot of trash he left behind and some cheap furniture."

"But you have photo ID," I protested.

"Yeah, but Greg Davis had long brown hair. Charles Sanford had fairly short bleached hair. Who knows what he looks like now? If he's holed up somewhere, then someone is bringing him food and supplies. We have an APB out on him. And we've done all the looking we know to do. Pestered the poor Balcombs to death."

"Who are they?"

"Parents of the girlfriend. They said Sandra came to see them, said everything was fine…but that was the same day as he tried to attack you. They haven't heard from her since."

"Didn't that worry them?"

"Nope. Apparently they're used to not hearing from her for days at a time, and then she appears all full of sunshine and family love. I don't understand it at all."

"So she wasn't at the apartment either?"

"Nope, no sign of her, except some cosmetics left behind, I guess they left in a hurry…after he attacked you. But where did they go?"

I had no answer to that, and I certainly didn't understand that girl—love of family didn't go with living with a scumbag like Davis/Sanford or whatever we were calling him. I decided she was more mixed up in her head than I was. When he fled, she must have known he was in trouble. Why didn't she go home?

I was sure Charles/Greg wasn't through with me. I was waiting for the next incident, large or small. Little things startled me—movement caught out of the corner of my eye, a tree branch falling as I walked down the driveway, a car that followed too close or so I thought.

"Kelly, you're turnin' into a pack of nerves," Keisha observed one day.

"You'd be nervous too, wouldn't you?"

"Shoot, I'm already nervous for you. Yes, I'd be nervous, but I know I can handle whatever that twerp does next. I admit it's a bit strange for him to be quiet so long, but I think that's part of it. Waiting makes you nervous. Remember, you've handled a lot of stuff, and you can handle this. You already have a couple of times."

That bolstered me a lot, and I resolved to walk with my head held high instead of creeping around corners.

Chapter Nine

By mid-morning Thanksgiving, I had the situation under control—buffet set with plates, silverware, wine glasses, etc. Serving dishes out on the dining table with little notes in them about what was to go in each. Mike had started smoking the turkey in the early hours, and I had put the roast turkey—a large one—in so that it would come out about two in the afternoon, which was when guests were scheduled to arrive. I had my list of who was bringing what—Keisha, sweet potato casserole; Claire, mashed potatoes; Joe and Theresa, Mexican salsas and chips; Anthony, store-bought rolls; Mom, her famous Italian cream cake, two of them; and Keisha's mom, her wonderful pumpkin chiffon pie. The girls were busy making the green-bean casserole—I cautioned them that we wouldn't put the traditional fried onion rings on until the last minute.

I heard Mike's cell ring but paid no attention. I was sorting through the cupboard where I knew there must be cocktail napkins and plates but darned if I could find them.

Mike burst into the kitchen. "Gotta go, Kelly. I'm so sorry. No idea when I'll be back."

"What's so important on Thanksgiving morning?"

"You know that girl that Greg Davis was beating? Her parents finally filed a missing persons report—still haven't heard from her. And so far, we haven't found him, let alone her."

My heart sank down to my toes, and I looked at Maggie, so calmly draining canned green beans, for once working in harmony with her sister who was pulling out casserole dishes.

"What about the turkey?" I nodded my head toward the backyard.

"Should be okay. Ask Joe if he can come check it about noon and then again at two when he gets here. Thermometer is out there. Smells divine."

I could agree with that, but I hated, just purely hated, the thought of that girl missing on a family holiday. And I wasn't much more thrilled with Mike being gone during the flurry of last-minute preparations.

He wasn't gone five minutes when Keisha called. "I'm comin' over to help you. Mike rousted José out even though he worked last night. It's apparently an all-hands search for that poor child."

"I think we're all right," I said, without much assurance in my voice. "I'm going to call Joe to check the turkey on the smoker."

"You don't need Joe," she scoffed. "I know how to smoke a turkey. I'll just have to leave to get Momma when the time comes."

And so she arrived, dressed to the nines, in a navy—I don't know what you'd call it, but it was loose and flowing and looked wonderful on her, and it had silver sparkles all over it. Silver sparkled in her hair and on her fingernails, and even Em was overwhelmed.

"Keisha, you look...you look like a princess!"

"That's me, sweetie," she said, planting a kiss of her forehead. Then she reached for Maggie, who, as she often did these days, instinctively drew away, then remembered herself and let Keisha wrap her arms around her.

"Precious baby," Keisha said, her voice anything but gentle, "we're going to keep you safe."

Maggie gave her a strange look, because she didn't know a thing about the missing girl, and I wasn't about to tell her.

The girls finally finished the casserole and put it into the space I'd cleared on top of the fridge in the stoop. As cold as it was outside, it would be fine without actual refrigeration. Keisha plugged in her slow cooker with its sweet potato casserole and dumped a bag of veggies on the counter. "I'm making a vegetable tray," she announced and began slicing celery, radishes, opening cans of olives, and the like.

I had kind of frozen in mid-action, unsure of what I was doing or why, my mind so totally focused on the missing girl. "Why can't they find that Greg Davis?"

I started toward my cell phone that lay on the kitchen table, but she stopped me. "You don't go bothering Mike. He'll call when he can. He knows you're upset, we're all upset." Then with an abrupt swing to efficiency, she said, "I got to go check that turkey."

She was back in a few minutes to report that it was doing just fine. I was glad I'd done so much preparation in advance, because I simply couldn't concentrate, couldn't go from one task to another. Keisha almost directed me, as I got soft drinks, beer and bottled water into two large coolers. Then she went off to get ice, muttering, "I sure will be glad when Maggie's old enough to drive and do errands like this."

My heart clutched. Today I didn't want Maggie out of my sight. Keisha saw the look and said, "Oh, not today. I wouldn't let her go today, but by the time she's sixteen, it will be safe."

I prayed she was right. I thought fleetingly about that child with no immunity who was raised in a bubble. I wanted to put my girls in a bubble.

Mike finally called at one-thirty. "I won't be home for dinner. You'll have to manage without me."

A corner of my mind registered that he thought I was capable of that, and I was pleased, because I knew I was. But the rest of me was crying out to learn about the girl. He was terse but as thorough as he could be. He said he had nothing new, and then my heart nearly stopped when he said, "I sure hope we don't find a murder/suicide deal."

I thought back to the Charles Sanford who'd tried to kill me and said, "I don't think so, but I'm terrified for the girl." Charles Sanford, or Greg Davis, wasn't the kind to do away with himself. Nor was he the kind to be that lovesick. No, the girl was in trouble.

****

By two it was cloudy and raining, as Keisha, the girls and I waited for our guests to arrive. Keisha put on Mike's raincoat to go get the smoked turkey, and I sent Maggie with an umbrella to shield the bird, not either of them. So far it was a gentle rain, the much-needed soaking kind, but rumbling thunder and occasional bolts of lightning threatened something more severe to come.

With everyone confined to the house, it was a bit crowded, and I could tell by the spirit of my guests that they all missed Mike and were aware that something big was keeping him away. Their inquiries were subtle, but I vowed to myself not to say anything. So comments like, "Hate for Mike to be missing this," or, "I hope he's not out in this weather," simply got a nod from me.

Maggie pulled me aside and whispered, "Tell me the truth. Where is Mike?" She was the last one I was going to tell about a missing teenage girl.

"Not now," I whispered back. "Later." I hoped she'd forget but I knew that was a vain hope.

Without Mike, there was a squabble about who would carve. Anthony was a good carpenter, but I had no idea what he knew about turkey, and I was quite sure Otto knew nothing. Claire stepped in. "I can carve a turkey. Give me the knife and the sharpener." And she cut it like a pro—cutting each half of the breast off in one large piece and then slicing it into nice pieces. While she carved, Keisha made gravy. As usual, the turkey was cold by the time we served it but the side dishes were hot, and everyone piled plates high. Then we sat around the living room, eating quietly without much conversation. Too quietly I thought.

My thoughts were on Sandra whatever her name was…and her family. They must be frantic, and I looked around the room thinking how blessed I was to be enjoying a turkey dinner with these people. It dawned on me that if Greg Davis/Charles Sanford had his way, I wouldn't be sitting here tonight—or was he just trying to scare me?

Stop it, Kelly. This is not about you! It's about a missing teenage girl. That thought made me turn to Maggie, who was politely carrying on a conversation with her grandmother and Otto, though I imagined not much about the conversation intrigued Maggie. Still I was grateful she was safely in our midst.

"Kelly, when do we find out if the baby is a boy or a girl?"

Pulled back to reality, I patted my swelling belly and said, "At least another month. They tell me sonograms hurt the baby's ears, so I don't want any more than necessary. They'll do one to check the baby's growth and make sure all is well. That's enough for me."

My mother sniffed. "In my day, we never knew until the baby

arrived. You were supposed to be a boy, Kelly. I had a blue nursery all ready."

"Maybe that's why I like blue," I said gently.

Somehow the evening passed, though I think guests left more quickly than usual. They sensed the tension in the air. Keisha and Claire stayed to clean up, but Claire left when we were almost through. "You two can handle this. Got to go." With an air kiss, she was out the door.

We finished the kitchen—it looked like no one had eaten, except for the dishes in the draining basket—but I had a refrigerator full of leftovers. I'd sent some with Claire and had some ready for Keisha.

"Put them outside," she said. "I'm not goin' anywhere until Mike comes home."

"Keisha! That might be three in the morning. You can't do that...and I can't stay awake that long."

"No matter. I'll sleep on the couch."

Em stuck her head around the corner. "I'll sleep on a pallet, Keisha. You can have my bed."

Keisha held out her arms. "Now aren't you the sweetest baby. Thanks, darlin'. I'll take you up on that."

So we fixed Em a pallet and got her a blanket. When we enlarged the house, I thought I was through fixing pallets, but I guess not.

Maggie was silent as we got out blankets and pillows, but finally she asked, "Keisha, why are you staying? Are you worried about Mom or are you worried about that girl?"

"What girl?" I asked. I hadn't yet explained the situation to her.

"I told her," Keisha said. "She needs to know what happens out there in the world." Then, turning to Maggie, she said simply, "Both. I'll feel better if I'm here."

I felt like I failed in my motherly duties. "Her name is Sandra, and I can only imagine how frightened her family is."

I held out my arms to welcome her into a hug, but Maggie shrugged and said, "They shouldn't have let her live with that guy. I'd never do that."

I guess that was a relief, but the rebuff of my hug stung. Instead, I got a hug from Keisha who whispered, "Hang in there, Kelly. It's gonna be all right."

"With the Sandra girl?" I asked.

She shook her head. "No. I got a bad feeling about that. But it's gonna be all right with Maggie."

I wasn't sure whether to smile or cry.

Mike came in about three—wet, cold, and weary. He peeled off his clothes, kissed me gently, and muttered, "I need a hot shower."

How romantic was that? By the time he was back, I had drifted off and was only barely aware that he wrapped his arms around me and fell asleep. I hadn't even gotten to ask any more about the murder/suicide theory.

Next morning, the girls hovered and listened to our every word, so it was not the time to talk about more than what to do with the long empty day. Maggie of course suggested mall shopping, but Mike and I both ignored her idea. I hated the mall any day of the year, but particularly the day after Thanksgiving. Keisha left early to go home and meet José, though the Grill would be closed and who knew where they would eat lunch.

Mike said he was going to work briefly but would be home for turkey sandwiches and would call if he couldn't make it.

****

At lunch, we sat around the table, with the girls obviously hearing our conversation. Once again, we had decided to hide nothing from them. Sandra Balcomb was one of two daughters of a couple who lived in neighboring Frisco Heights. "Nice people, modest house, but they work hard. Dad's a mail carrier, mom teaches school. Probably in their early fifties. They're torn up about this."

I wanted to ask why, then, did they let her live with her boyfriend, which seemed unconscionable to me. Mike must have seen the question in my eyes.

"They said she's always been headstrong, threatened to run away if they didn't let her stay with him. They don't like Greg—that's how they know him—one bit. Say she may be headstrong but she's a good girl, gone to church all her life, and on and on."

"Is she an only child?"

"No. And here's what's weird—in fact, I'm puzzling, trying to piece this together. Her older sister, Janice, still lives at home. She's twenty-four, but she's the receptionist at Dr. Goodwin's clinic. That young girl I thought was so pretty and charming. She stayed home today, and she sure didn't look as pretty and chipper as she did at the clinic."

"How did they know Sandra's missing? You knew days ago she wasn't at the apartment, and they were used to not hearing from her. So why the big panic all of a sudden?"

"A phone call. She tried to call and wish them a happy Thanksgiving, said she was sorry not to be there....when someone grabbed the phone and disconnected the call. Janice was the one who talked to her, but she's pretty tight-lipped, says she erased it from her call listing because she's afraid for her sister."

"And that set off the mass search yesterday?" I asked.

"Yeah. They were afraid for her life, and frankly so was I."

"You mean," Maggie asked, "you thought she might have been killed."

Em grabbed her sister's arm and held on tight.

"That's exactly what I mean, Mags. Her parents called, left messages, for several days. Say she usually comes by in the afternoon after school on her way to her after-school job at a yogurt place and always comes on holidays. Finally the dad did what we did. He went to Greg's place and found it empty. Found just what we did—he'd moved out, no clue where he went."

"What can you do?"

"We put out an Amber Alert on Sandra—at seventeen, she's barely eligible. But we can't do a thing about finding Greg, except pray for a break, and that worries me. He's loose, out there, and for some reason he has this big grudge or something against you. When we find Greg, I suspect we'll find Sandra. I only hope she's safe and unharmed."

The girls were silent, but Em's eyes were wild. A fleeting thought went through my mind that this was a tough but good lesson about growing up in a world with lots of dangers.

"And Greg now has a loose tie to my doctor's office. Somehow this all has to fit together—Greg Davis, whoever he is, Dr. Goodwin's office, my pregnancy, maybe the inheritance from Robert Martin."

"If the inheritance were part of it, I'd zero in on Jo Ellen North. But nothing I hear about her sounds promising. She's apparently a model prisoner."

I sighed. Memories of Jo Ellen holding a gun on me and trying to choke me came flooding back. "She's conniving. We know that. Maybe she's just biding her time, and the inheritance pushed her over the edge."

"Sweetheart, I think you're letting your imagination run away with you. Remember our deal—you handle the personal stuff, the emotional side of things. I'll take care of detective work. And I will keep you safe."

Mike's cell indicated a text message. He read it and said, "Got to go. See you tonight."

I sat and stewed. He'd as much as patted me on the head and told me to be a good girl. I had been treated condescendingly, and I was properly indignant. But then something he said about taking care of the people part struck me. I got out the phone book and located the Balcombs on Frazier, close to the high school. Then I called Mona and asked if the girls could both stay at Bun Appetit while I ran an errand. Of course, she agreed, and the girls were ecstatic. I delivered them and headed for the grocery store where I bought a sliced meat tray, a fruit tray, and a Bundt cake. Then I headed for Frazier Avenue.

The Balcomb home was a small frame cottage, probably two bedrooms and one bath. It had been painted not too many years ago, off white with a medium blue trim and shutters. A picket fence marked the edges of the property, and a concrete walk led to the porch where bright yellow mums added a nice touch of color. The people who lived here cared for their house.

As I walked to the porch, carrying my grocery sack, I thought I saw a sheer curtain in one front window move a bit. Almost as soon as I rang the bell, the door opened a crack and a woman said, "I'm sorry. This is not a good time."

I used Mike's technique and put my foot out so she couldn't close the door, trusting she wouldn't be forceful. At the same time, I said, "Please. I know about Sandra. I'm here to help."

She opened the door a little more, and I saw a face haggard with worry and fear. "Help? I don't know how anyone can help." She wiped away a tear.

In a minute, she'd have me bawling. "Please, Mrs. Balcomb. I'm Kelly O'Connell. My husband is Officer Mike Shandy. I know you've talked to him yesterday and today."

She perked up just a bit. "He's a kind man, a good man. I just hope he can find Sandra in time."

I didn't ask in time for what? "May I come in? I brought some food because I was sure you wouldn't feel like cooking." I thrust the grocery bag toward her.

"How kind of you, a total stranger. The neighbors haven't even been over to see what we need." She opened the door wider and said, "Please do come in. I'm sure you understand we're not at our best."

"Of course," I said. "Your neighbors probably don't even know what happened. It hasn't been in the paper or on TV, though I expect it will be today." All of a sudden, I ran out of talk. I wondered why I was there, what I wanted to ask or say, what I expected to accomplish. And yet at the same time I felt a bond with these people.

She showed me into a small living room, crowded with a couch and two large recliners, now upright, the usual TV, and tired drapery that hung sadly at the edge of the sheers in each of the windows. Beyond I could see a round oak dining table—probably an antique—covered with a lace cloth. The inside was like the outside—clean and neat but in need of updating.

Framed photographs covered a side table, some showing two young girls together, others chronicling the girls' growth as they progressed through school. "Which is the most current of Sandra?" I asked.

Wordlessly, she handed me a picture, and I studied it. She was pretty but not striking, her streaky blond hair cut into what in my day was called a pixie or something similar—today's version of the spiky haircut. She wore a tad too much makeup, a photographer's black drape top, and stared at the camera with an enigmatic look. I couldn't tell if she could be sassy or sweet. As I handed the picture back, I said, "Pretty girl."

"She can be," Mrs. Balcomb said with a sigh.

Mr. Balcomb shuffled into the room—he was not old, but today he walked with the shuffle and bent shoulders of an old man the world had beaten down. His wife whispered to him, no doubt about who I was and the food I'd brought, and he came forward, now a bit more erect, to take my hand in both of his. "You're very kind. Please sit down. Alma, can we at least serve coffee?"

I held up a hand. "No, thank you. I just finished lunch. I don't need anything."

I sat on the couch, and they each sat in overstuffed chairs that were probably his and hers, where they spent hours watching TV. For a moment, there was an awkward silence.

"I am so sorry about Sandra," I said. "I have a teenage daughter, younger, but still I can't imagine what you're going through."

"We shouldn't have let her stay with that young man," the mother said. She studied the carpet and avoided eye contact with me. "We...I...was so afraid that she'd end up on the streets, I thought it was better to keep her in communication with us."

I thought for a moment. "I think you're right, but I can't say what I'd do in a situation like that. My daughter, so far, is just beginning to be interested in boys. I wasn't wild about the first one she brought home, and I'm sure I'll be too critical."

"He's shifty-eyed," Mr. Balcomb said, "and he's got a limp handshake. I like a man with a firm grip. You can usually trust him."

A nervous giggle threatened to erupt—absolutely the wrong thing at this moment. But the idea of Greg Davis/Charles Sanford with a limp handshake somehow struck me as funny. I plunged in where I probably shouldn't have. "I've met him. Under unusual circumstances. But my husband said he was the same young man who beat your daughter a while back. I wonder she didn't take that as a warning."

"She didn't…but we did," the man said. "She told us about it. Had to explain the shiner. I told her to get out of there and come home. But she wouldn't listen."

"As the saying goes," Alma Balcomb said sadly, "she made her bed."

"Did they perhaps run away to get married?" I asked.

"Dear God, I hope not," was the response from the mother.

Just then Janice wandered into the room, saying, "Mom, don't…" She stopped, startled when she saw a stranger, but then almost instantly recognizing me. "Ms. O'Connell, what are you doing here?"

"I brought your family some food and came to share your worry," I said.

Mike was right. She wasn't the pretty, bright girl who greeted patients at Dr. Goodwin's office. Her face was pale, her eyes puffy, her hair in need of a shampoo. But even disheveled, she looked much more traditional than her younger sister—shoulder-length hair, jeans and a T-shirt. She was still skeptical about my presence. "How did you know?"

"My husband is commander with the Central Division of the police department. He remembers you from Dr. Goodwin's office, and he was here yesterday and today to talk to you."

"He remembers me?" For a moment, her face reflected pleasure at what she presumed was flattery, but then her expression changed. "He was here this morning with other officers. We told them everything we know. I don't think we have any more to tell you." Her body language gave off clear signs of tension.

Instinct shouted at me that she wasn't just tense over her missing sister. There was more to it, something she hadn't shared with her parents, even as she bent over to console her mom for what I presume was not the first time. Leaning toward her mother, she shot a wary glance in my direction.

"I'm not here to investigate—that's my husband's responsibility. I'm here because I hate that this is happening to a family in our community." Hah, there Mike Shandy. I hope she quotes that to you. In truth, I was a little uneasy about how Mike would take this visit, but hadn't he told me to take care of the emotional end of things?

She straightened and looked at me, still clutching her mother's hand. "I don't think we have anything to say to you."

I repeated, "I didn't come for information. I came to see if I could be of help, and I brought some food. That's what neighbors do when there's trouble in a family."

"We don't need charity."

At that, Alma Balcomb let go of her daughter's hand, rose from her chair, and demanded, "Janice Balcomb, where are your manners? You will not talk that way to a guest in our house."

With a muffled cry and a hand over her mouth, the daughter

turned and fled the room.

Mr. Balcomb—I hadn't yet learned his first name—mumbled, "She's upset. She and her sister were close."

I stood. "I don't want to cause more upset when I came to see if I could comfort." I drew a business card from my purse and handed it to Alma. "Please call me if I can do anything to help. I really mean that."

Alma looked at the card, then at me, and smiled weakly. "Thank you. I appreciate your kindness." She paused at minute, glanced in the direction her daughter had gone, and asked, "How does Janice know you?"

"I'm a patient of Dr. Goodwin's."

She nodded as if that cleared up a puzzle. "Such a nice woman, and such nice people in her clinic. We're grateful Janice has a job there."

I agreed Dr. Goodwin's clinic was a good place for a young girl to work, shook hands with Mr. Balcomb who had pushed himself out of his chair, and gave Mrs. Balcomb a hug. "I'm sorry if I upset Janice." And I was out the door and down the walk to my car. I didn't dare turn to look, but I bet those sheer curtains swayed slightly.

I drove back to Bun Appetit to get the girls, all the while wondering what was troubling Janice Balcomb. In fact, I thought troubling a slight term for it. That girl was afraid of something. Deathly afraid. For herself or for her sister?

And something else bothered me. If he was a postal carrier, she was a teacher, and Janice worked, I figured they had a combined income of $75,000 between the parents, and say Janice contributed even $12,000 a year—a thousand a month—they should be able to update their house. I knew some people just set up housekeeping once and never touched the place again, but little signs showed that these people cared about their house. Were they supporting Sandra? And her boyfriend? If so, why did they do it? Did he have some way to threaten them? Something was wrong—okay, that was my instinct again. Mike would never believe it. But he would believe me about Janice. That meant I had to tell him where I went this afternoon.

I was still pondering when I drove the girls home, despite their protests they wanted to stay at Bun Appetit longer. Em broke into my thoughts, "Mom, is something wrong?"

"No, sweetie. Not at all."

By the time we got home, I was stewing about what I'd fix for supper. Turkey hash made with dressing, gravy, and turkey.

As usual that night at the supper table, Mike asked how the day had gone for all of us. The girls reported on their visit to Bun Appetit, and Maggie said that she and Jenny wanted to have a sleepover at Jenny's next weekend. I said we'd discuss it.

Mike turned to me. "Sweetheart? How come the girls were at Bun Appetit? You need a nap?"

I took a swallow of water and said, "I went to visit the Balcombs today." I thought about saving this news until we were out of hearing of the girls, but then, it was a good lesson in compassion for them—or so my thinking went.

Mike's fork clattered to his plate. "You what?"

"I went to see the Balcombs."

"I didn't even tell you where they lived." He was incredulous, so much so that he forgot to ask why I went.

"They're in the phone book. Not hard, Mike." I was struggling for composure. "Remember at lunch you agreed I should take care of the people part, and you'd solve the crimes? So I did just that. I went to pay a call of compassion, and I took some food."

Maggie finally caught up with the conversation enough to ask, "Who are the Balcombs?"

Mike said shortly, "Just a minute, Maggie. Kelly, I didn't really mean it that way."

"Well, after you patted me on the head, I decided that was what you meant."

"I didn't pat you on the head. If I remember rightly, I kissed the top of your head."

"Mike, I think they were grateful. No neighbors had paid them kindness visits, and they're really beyond upset. And I sure wasn't putting myself in danger."

He thought a minute and finally said, "I guess not." Then he changed the subject. I knew the discussion wasn't over.

While I was doing dishes—Em's turn to dry—my cell phone rang. I answered with my usual, "Kelly O'Connell."

"Ms. O'Connell? This is Sally Buxton. I hope I'm not interrupting." Her voice was calm, caring, just like it was in the office.

"No, Mrs. Buxton. What can I do for you?"

"I'm so worried about Janice Balcomb, and I know your husband is investigating her sister's disappearance. I talked to Janice this afternoon. She said she doesn't think she'll be back in the office this week, which of course makes it difficult for us to serve our patients. But I really called because I am so worried about her. She didn't sound like herself at all."

I could agree with that. "I think she's terribly upset, afraid for her sister, worried about her parents. The whole family's taking it hard. I suspect she's staying home partly to be with her parents and take care of them."

"She sounded so distraught, I thought maybe she knew more than she was telling me."

"Not that I know of," I said. I didn't think it smart to confirm that had been my suspicion, too. "It's kind of you to call though."

"Well, you let me know if you hear anything, would you please?"

I assured her I would, and after a few questions about how I was feeling—I told her fine—she hung up with profuse thanks.

I stood there for a long time, phone in my hand. Was this just what it seemed—an innocent call of concern—or was it another piece to the puzzle? What possible connection could she have to Greg Davis or any of this mess?

Late that night, I told Mike the whole story, beginning with how strange Janice Balcomb acted.

He looked up from his book. "Instinct, Kelly?"

All right, I was a bit defensive. "Yes, instinct. Didn't you notice anything when you were there this morning?"

"Grief, yes. And worry. But nothing beyond that. Your imagination again, Kelly."

I loved this guy so much, but he could make me so mad. And when he did, it was because he dismissed me, didn't take me seriously. "You better go back in the morning and judge again," I said, turning my back on him.

My attempt at indignation was ruined, because I immediately turned around and said, "I forgot. Mrs. Buxton called tonight."

"Who is Mrs. Buxton?"

"The nurse practitioner from Dr. Goodwin's office. You know, the one who's always so solicitous."

"So why did she call? Are you having any symptoms you haven't told me about?"

"No, she called because she has the same instinct I do. She was worried about Janice Balcomb. Thought she was upset enough that we should be alarmed, wanted to know what I knew."

"How would she know you knew anything?"

"She talked to Janice this evening."

Mike suddenly threw his book across the room, a gesture totally unlike him. "This is getting out of hand. Everyone knows more about my case…or thinks they do…than I do. Kelly, do not go near the Balcombs again." He realized rather quickly that I'd resent being given a direct order that went counter to my nature, so he added, "Please? As a favor to me?"

"I'm not promising. But I'll wait a day or two and maybe Sandra will turn up." *And you'll cool down. Mike sees this as a straightforward missing person's case. I see it as a jigsaw puzzle in which, so far, the pieces don't fit at all.*

****

Sandra Balcomb's picture was on the front page of the morning paper. I glanced at it as I started breakfast for the girls, waiting for Mike to come make his world-class pancakes. Once I had a cup of coffee in front of me, I spread the paper out and read only the first sentence, because Keisha called and interrupted me.

"You read the newspaper about that poor girl?"

"Trying to," I replied with a big dose of sarcasm.

"What did her folks say yesterday? Now don't be so surprised. I knew where you'd go."

"I wasn't sleuthing. I went to pay a compassionate call and take some food, not to see what I could learn. That's Mike's job."

Keisha finally said, "That girl is scared out of her wits. But she's goin' to be all right."

"This is one time I really do hope your sixth sense is right on." I went back to reading the paper.

The article was basically a plea for anyone with information to come forward. Anonymous tips would be accepted at the police non-emergency number. There was a reward of $10,000 for any tip that led to Sandra's safe return to her family. Then it deteriorated into an account of Sandra's life, which was relatively unremarkable. She attended local schools and was a senior at Paschal High, scheduled to graduate in May. Good student, not active in extracurricular activities but a member of the local Church of Christ and attended regularly. Nothing in the article about her living with her boyfriend or having a slightly rebellious streak.

A mug shot of Greg Davis topped a sidebar, listing him as a person of interest, known to be close to Sandra and probably the last person she was seen with. Greg Davis did not resemble Charles Sanford. He had apparently cleaned himself up for his gig as Sanford—shaved off a stubble of beard, cut his below-the-ear hair into a conventional style and bleached it, and spiffed up his wardrobe, changing from what looked like jailhouse orange to a suit. Who is Greg Davis? Where did he come from? What's his stake in all this, because it goes far beyond a romantic relationship, even an obsession with Sandra Balcomb? She had nothing to do with the rest of the puzzle, as far as I could tell.

The thought went through my mind that both Greg Davis and Sandra Balcomb were self-serving, not passionate lovers devoted to each other. Bonnie and Clyde they were not.

Chapter Eleven

Maybe I let my guard down, but I'd been thinking that since Greg Davis was missing and presumably hiding out somewhere deep and dark, I was safe from both harassment and serious attacks on my well-being or that of my family. I was taking advantage of my pregnancy, though I didn't even admit that to Keisha. But as I had threatened, I stayed home one day a week, usually Friday to gear up for the weekend when we always seemed to have extra people around, more mouths to feed, and I was in the kitchen a lot, especially since the weather was too cold to grill.

Usually I tried to devote part of Friday morning to office work and part to weekend planning, menus and the like. And then I took a nice nap before it was time to get the girls. But one Friday in early December, my planning was devoted to Christmas—gifts, schedule, the whole works. Claire had invited us to Christmas dinner, so I could cross that off my list except for the dressing, green beans, and wine I'd promised to bring, the latter being Mike's end of the responsibilities. But every year my gift list grew—I liked to give something nice to Keisha, and this year a joint gift to her and José would be appropriate. But then there were Mom and Claire and Anthony, with token gifts to Claire's girls and Anthony's children, and Mom's paramour, Otto. The term struck me as hilarious, and I laughed out loud. And then Joe and Theresa, and this year I wanted to have something for baby Lorna. Plus of course Mike and the girls. It made my head spin, and I worked until almost noon.

Then I fixed myself a peanut butter sandwich—I seemed to crave peanut butter these days—and a glass of milk. Got to keep that calcium up for baby bones! I went back upstairs, read for maybe ten minutes and fell asleep. It was a good thing I'd set the alarm for 2:45 because it brought me out of a sound sleep. I could pick up the girls in the sweats I slept in, since I didn't have to get out of the car, so I shoved my feet into tennis shoes and headed downstairs to grab keys and phone off the kitchen table where I'd left them.

Propped against the salt and peppers was a note on white paper. In crude block lettering, it said, "Hope you had a nice nap. Didn't want to disturb you—this time."

I screamed, a long, blood-curdling scream. Then I called Mike, who said not to touch anything and he'd be right home. Next I called Keisha to get the girls—she thanked me for the advance notice, but I didn't tell her what was wrong. She'd find out when she got here.

And then, with the necessary people notified, I sat down and had a good cry, from which I retreated only long enough to check the doors—all locked—and the alarm system—fully armed. How had someone gotten into the house in spite of all our safety precautions? And how did I, who considered myself a light sleeper, sleep through the intrusion? Hours later, in retrospect, I decided it was a good thing I slept rather than attempting a confrontation or simply scaring myself out of my wits.

Mike found me sitting at the kitchen table, still in a daze, eyes red from crying. I pointed to the note without saying anything, and he nodded to the officer with him to bag it. Then he pulled me over onto his lap, ignoring the junior grade officer who was trying hard not to look at us.

Mike stroked my hair and rubbed my back, and I began to sob all over again. "How," I managed to gulp, "did Greg Davis manage to get in here. The house was secure—I checked."

"I know," Mike soothed. "I checked too."

"And he's on the run or hiding out. How could he come here?"

"Kelly, we don't know that it was him, and if it was all I can say is he has a lot of nerve…and some skills we didn't know about, like lock picking and disarming alarm systems."

When Mike's guys investigated, they found whoever broke in had disconnected the alarm system so it didn't go off but later had rewired it so it appeared intact.

"Damn clever," Mike muttered in reluctant admiration. "He's a petty crook with some undesirable skills. Bet he can pick pockets too."

The troops also discovered where he'd picked the lock on the back door, and Mike resolved to improve the security of that door. Seemed to me it was locking the barn door after the horse was out—or in, in this case.

By the time Keisha brought the girls home, the house seemed to be crawling with police officers. Well, not really, there were only two plus Mike, but it seemed like an army.

Maggie and Em rushed to me, with cries of "Mom, are you all right?" "What happened?" I hugged them, and looked at Keisha who took in my puffy eyes and raised a questioning eyebrow at me.

"We've had an incident," I said and found my voice was shaky. But downplaying it as much as I could I told them about the note.

Em's look was one of pure terror. "He was in our house? I'm

sleeping on the floor in your room tonight."

Maggie played a more sophisticated role. "He didn't do anything, did he? It was just, as Mom says, harassment. But Mom's brought danger home to us again." She stalked off to her room.

Thank you, Maggie. If she spent Saturday night at Jenny's, there was no way Em would sleep downstairs alone. But I put that thought off for the time being.

Mike's guys found nothing else of interest—no fingerprints, etc.,—so they left with Mike's blessing and my gratitude. I was exhausted. I heard Mike on his cell phone and figured out he was talking to Anthony. "Yes, two 4x4s. You measure how long it needs to be. Front and back."

"What was that about?" I asked.

"You ever hear how settlers used to protect against Indians?" he countered.

I sighed. Perhaps Mike had been reading too much early Texas history, his special interest. "No, how?"

"They put brackets up on either side of a door and then put a large board, say 4x4, across them, effectively blocking the door from being broken down. So it wouldn't matter if our guy can pick the lock."

Several thoughts swirled through my mind, the first that it certainly was not an aesthetic way to improve the atmosphere of the house. Ugly is the word I had in mind. The second was that it would be awkward, hoisting that board up and down. "Just the back door?"

"Nope, all exterior doors. Course we only have the two."

He seemed completely cheerful about his great idea, while I was wondering how heavy the board was and whether or not I could lift it when I was nine months pregnant. Or could Em lift it if necessary? What if there was a fire?

"Mike, can we talk about this?" I outlined my objections, but he had his answers ready.

"We'll have practice sessions with the girls, and if you lift the boards every day, you should be able to do it. Good exercise for you."

I wondered how bad it would be if I kicked him, hard, under the table.

"Kelly, my most important duty is to see that you and the girls are safe. Now that we know this guy's ability, this seems the only way. I'll call the security company tomorrow—surely they're open on Saturdays—and have them check the system, see what they can do about beefing up the alarm that's supposed to sound outdoors. I suspect they'll tell us to get a land line—then when service is disrupted, the alarm will go off in the house."

"Mike, if this guy is out of hiding enough to leave this note, why can't your people find him? You've got strong charges against him— threatening me with a knife and kidnapping Sandra Balcomb."

He was patient, infuriatingly so. "We have no proof that Greg Davis broke in here today. And for all we know Sandra Balcomb may have run to get away from him, her parents, who knows what? The only thing we have is your word that you felt threatened by Charles Sanford."

"Felt? I was threatened!" This conversation was not going well, and I longed for a glass of wine.

It was a tense weekend at our house. Friday night, with Maggie's semi-gracious permission, Em put a pallet in her sister's room and slept there. She said she didn't sleep all night, but Maggie scoffed and said she snored most of the night. Saturday night Maggie went to Jenny's, after Jenny's mom promised me she'd be home all evening, and Em moved her pallet upstairs to our room.

Sunday Anthony installed the brackets and boards on the doors, but he had taken the time to paint the one for the back door to match the kitchen and stain the one for the front door as close as he could to the color of the door. I still thought they were eyesores, but I told him I was grateful.

"Miss Kelly, we got to keep you safe."

I lifted the boards into place and put them back down, but they were heavy, and I knew they'd get heavier as I grew larger and heavier myself. Em to our delight dragged the kitchen stool over and easily put the board in place and then removed it. Maggie had to show her superior strength and did it without the stool, but she almost dropped it when she was taking it out of the brackets. When not in use the boards would rest next to their doors. Not my idea of decorating.

I couldn't vent my feelings that all this protection was the wrong approach. Yes, I wanted to be safe, and I was grateful when Mike was home. But finding out where Greg Davis was and why he was stalking me and how the pieces of the puzzle fit together was what we must do in order to get this episode over with.

And yet, because I wanted to feel safe, always, I even considered giving up my Fridays at home. With Christmas looming there was so much to be done. On Sunday, I sat the girls down at the kitchen table with paper and pencil and told them to make their Santa Claus wish list. Since both of them were too old to believe in Santa, they gave me weird looks but they bent to their task. Maggie asked to use my computer to look up some things she wanted, and I told her to write down the URL.

But as I went through the motions of being normal—helping the girls, cooking Sunday supper—anxiety loomed like a dark cloud over my head.

****

I didn't share this with Mike, but I was convinced that Robert Martin's will had a lot to do with my stalker, the puzzle in my head, and all the bad things going on. So Monday morning I called Benjamin Cruze of Bachman and Bannister.

When I identified myself, he immediately said in cordial tones, "Good morning, Ms. O'Connell. I have nothing new to report. I know you'd probably like to have your money, but as of now I have no progress to report. We're researching the claim of the person who disputes the inheritance."

"No, Benjamin," I said. He could be formal if he wanted. It wasn't my style. "That's not why I'm calling. How does one person have any grounds to contest? If no one knows who's included and who inherits what, how can there be a complaint?" I was pushing him out of his comfort zone.

He stammered. "Well…uh…it's an unusual situation. Ah…rather long and complicated."

"I'm in no hurry," I said.

"Well, this person had access to the will as it was originally written but has never seen it as he amended it in his later years."

"And?" I prompted.

He was careful. "This person has figured out that will was changed and someone else inherits rather than the single person in the original version. The person…."

I kept waiting for him to slip and say he or she, but he disappointed me.

"…does now know about specific bequests. There may have

been a slip before we knew...."

"Knew what?"

"Uh, exactly who we were dealing with."

I pushed. "If you can't tell me who this person is, then how do they know who I am? It doesn't take a lot of imagination to figure out who the original sole beneficiary was. But no one would ever dream that Robert Martin would name me in his will, let alone so generously."

His voice was tight. "As I said, there was a slip."

I could envision him, sitting at a lawyerly desk and turning beet red with embarrassment. "One more question: if this contest or however you say it goes to court, will the will be open to all who are named?"

"If the judge orders it." This time he was on firm ground. "We hope it will not come to that."

"I think you've told me all I need to know. Thank you, Benjamin." I hung up and let out the breath I'd been holding.

"Robert Martin's will is at the center of this whole thing," I announced to Keisha, "and Jo Ellen North is contesting the will."

"And you know that how?"

"Sixth sense," I said grinning. "But I still have a puzzle."

And I began to draw a chart on a legal pad. I put Robert Martin's will in one column and under it Jo Ellen North. In another column I put Greg Davis and under that Sandra Balcomb and then, after a moment's hesitation, Janice Balcomb with a question mark. Was Janice afraid of Greg? Afraid for Sandra? Had she heard from one or both of them? Then there was Sarah Buxton—did she belong on my chart or not? I put her in a separate column and drew an arrow to Janice.

I went back and circled Greg Davis' name? Where did he come from? How did he fit into this whole thing?

I stewed over those scribblings for an hour until Keisha asked, "You figurin' anything out?"

"No. Let's go eat lunch. That new pizza place where Mike and I took the girls the other day."

"That on your diet?"

"It is today," I said, grabbing my purse.

Keisha took her time about sliding her feet out of her flip-flops and into her spiky heels, gathering her purse, and generally getting ready to go. As she stood she looked at me and said, "Kelly, it's all gonna work out. Be of good faith."

For the first time I wasn't so sure about her sixth sense.

At lunch, she totally changed the subject. "Now about the wedding. José says the sooner the better."

That caught me so by surprise that I gave a small gasp, which caused Keisha to give me one of her long looks. I'd been thinking the wedding would be, oh, April, and by then I'd have Greg Davis and Sandra Balcomb and contested inheritances off my mind.

"Is that a problem?" Keisha asked, her voice sharper than usual.

Who was I to delay her lifelong dream? "No, course not. It just took me by surprise. When do you want to have it?"

"Well, Christmas is almost upon us...."

Since this was the sixteenth of December, I'd say yes it was. I felt smug that my Christmas shopping was mostly done, Christmas Eve and Christmas dinner plans were made, and everything was falling into place. In the back of my mind, I was so much more prepared in advance because I didn't want Greg Davis to ruin our holiday. And I couldn't believe the Balcomb family would have to worry through the Christmas holiday.

Keisha looked at me and knew my thought had wandered off. "Kelly, you listenin' to me?"

The waiter interrupted. I ordered a caprese salad and Keisha had a Margherita pizza, declaring she'd take half home to José. Then she went on as though we hadn't been interrupted and I hadn't lost the train of thought.

"José says late January."

"That's barely a month away. Can we pull it all together by then? I mean what about invitations, showers, all that kind of stuff."

"I got an email list of those I want to invite. I'll design it real pretty and send it out."

I really did gasp then. "Email wedding invitations?"

"It's my wedding," she said firmly, "and I'm saving money—and now time—where I can. I'll ask for RSVPs and those that don't reply will get a call from me demanding to know if they're coming or not."

I was truly appalled. Keisha always lived and operated outside the box, but this was a bit much for me, and I couldn't imagine my mother's reaction to an email wedding invitation. In fact, I didn't want to imagine it. So I swallowed and said, "Okay."

"And those who want to give me a bridal shower"—she pointed a meaningful finger at me—"can do so after the fact or maybe the day before. We settled on a date—Sunday, the twenty-fifth—and I checked with both Mona and Peter. They're ready to go—Peter suggests salads as appetizers—he can do a variety as you know—and he'll do fried mozzarella, fried pickle chips, curly fries, and onion rings. And Mona's excited about bringing her whole array of hot dog choices. The two of them had a wonderful time planning this event. So that's all set, and the date is fine with them."

"So what do I need to do?" I was really confused here. As it turns out, she had so many chores for me, I needed pencil and paper.

"First, help me word the invitation."

No problem. I wrote that down.

"Second, help me shop for a dress."

There I balked a bit. I wasn't a fashionista, and my preference for jeans, loafers and a corduroy jacket certainly ran counter to Keisha's flamboyant taste. "Wouldn't Claire be better at that?" Claire kept up with the latest styles.

Keisha shook her head. "Nope. You, Maggie, Em and I are going shopping together. We got to find something we all like. We won't find it in bridal shops. I'm thinkin' Pink Ice or Lulu's for the girls…."

I carefully wrote those names down.

"And Zulilly's for me."

"I've never heard of any of those."

"Online shopping, Kelly. Only way to go. Only we got to hurry to make sure everything fits in time."

Email invitations and online shopping for wedding clothes? Since online shopping was my favorite anyway, I guessed I could accommodate and I'd have to shop that way for a dress for me if I wanted a new one.

Keisha did it to me again. "You can wear pants if you want."

I collected myself. "Cake?"

"Swiss Pastry Shop—Black Forest. No groom's cake. Hey, this day is all about me!"

It certainly seemed that way. That was a switch because she'd originally talked about two cakes, but I didn't bring that up. We went back to the office, my head scrambling to sort all this out. Once there I pulled up the websites Keisha had mentioned. Some of the outfits for young girls were outrageous and I'd never let my girls wear them, but I did find a few bright-colored dresses that might work. They were outlandishly short but I guessed I had to get used to that. When I pulled up Lane & Bryant, I found the choices dull and discouraging. So I began to doodle on a wedding invitation. Finally I handed it to Keisha:

Keisha Johnson and Joseph Thornberry
Invite you to share the joy of their
wedding day
Sunday, January twenty-sixth
The Old Neighborhood Grill
Four o'clock in the afternoon

Keisha took one look and said, "His name is José. That's how my friends know him."

I bit my tongue to keep from asking about his friends. I'd never met any and didn't know if he had a life apart from Keisha these days.

Chapter Twelve

As Christmas moved inevitably closer, I felt I was living in suspended animation. The Balcombs, however, were living in tension, longing, and hope mixed with despair. There had been no word from Sandra, no record of her. With Mike's blessing—he'd changed his mind on that issue—I visited the family once or twice, taking with me gifts—a poinsettia, a basket of cheese and sausage, and once, a smoked turkey.

They were grateful, pitifully grateful. Somehow I doubted they'd moved much from their chairs in the living room but sat day after day, not speaking because what was there to say? They watched newscasts with the dedication of religious zealots but deep down, they knew if there was any news, they'd have heard it first from the police.

To what I hoped was my credit, I didn't try to cheer them. How could you do that to people for whom life held no cheer? When I once offered to pray with them, they willingly agreed and so I, who had been derelict in church attendance for many years, found myself beseeching the Lord to bring Sandra safely home and to bless all of us. Our brief prayers—and I really did try to enlarge on the message—became a ritual for us.

I visited on December 23 and learned that neighbors had invited them to Christmas dinner. They would go, they said, but I didn't imagine they'd add much joy, and I blessed the neighbors in my mind.

Janice had long since returned to work. I had a regular check-up appointment with Mrs. Buxton the day after my mind-boggling lunch with Keisha. Janice was subdued when she greeted me and asked me to have a seat in the waiting area. I watched as other patients came in and noted that she was a bit more lively greeting them—but she wasn't back to the personable girl who had so impressed Mike. And occasionally I saw her cast a furtive glance in my direction. I truly doubted she was much comfort to her grieving parents.

Mrs. Buxton was her usual concerned self, asking "How are we feeling?" and declaring my weight and vital signs all perfect, except for my blood pressure, which was high enough to worry her. She asked about depression, and I answered with a firm denial. Why bother her with worry about Greg Davis and the inheritance and even the missing girl, though I'm sure she worried enough about that herself, with daily contact with Janice Balcomb. To distract her, I prattled on about the upcoming wedding while she brusquely tried to concentrate on measurements and heart rate and all those other things she had to check. Both the baby and I proved to be in great shape, and the ultrasound showed that we would have another baby girl. I decided I'd save that bit of news for Christmas morning with Mike and the girls, and I held it close to me like a precious gift. I knew there would be much clamoring over the name, but I already began to think of names I liked.

The blood pressure bothered me enough that I stopped at a drugstore and bought one of those gadgets that lets you take it at home. I did, and it was 118/70. Why was it always higher when Mrs. Buxton took it? I'd be taking it at home once a week from now on.

****

My hope that Greg Davis would release Sandra Balcomb before

Christmas was false, though I was still sure he held her. Mike kept telling me no body was a positive sign, a bit of comfort I never repeated to the Balcombs.

But neither did Greg leave us alone for a peaceful Christmas. The letter arrived in the office mail on December 23, addressed to Kelly O'Connell. Plain white envelope, address typed in the old Courier font that nobody uses these days. The uneven inking of the letters suggested to me that it had actually been typed on a very old manual typewriter with an almost worn-out ribbon. I was hesitating when Keisha peered over my shoulder and commanded, "Don't open that!"

I dropped the letter and looked at her.

"And don't touch it again. Call Mike."

"Oh, really. Isn't that a big fuss over nothing?"

"That letter strike you as strange? You see a return address on it?"

I sat staring at it and then lifted the phone to call Mike. He backed up Keisha's instinct, though he would have said it was police training that led him to say, "Don't touch it again. For all you know, Kelly, it could have anthrax in it."

Oh, good. Give me a new something to worry about that I hadn't thought of yet! Without touching the letter I looked for traces of white powder around it but saw none. It seemed to take Mike forever to get there, and I supposed as long as I followed orders there was no rush. But I couldn't do any work with that letter square in the middle of my desk. Besides, my mind wouldn't concentrate.

Keisha tried to distract me. "You got everything done for Christmas? Where you all gonna be tomorrow night?"

I had to think about what tomorrow night was. But then I said,

"My mom wants to host a small gathering—just us and Otto." I wasn't really too thrilled at the idea, and I bet Mom would serve oyster stew, a tradition she and my dad enjoyed and I hated. I could just see my girls reacting to oyster stew. Out of politeness and to keep my mind busy, I asked Keisha, "What are you and José going to do?"

"My mom and his folks are coming to us. I'm going to serve an enchilada casserole, rice and beans, nachos, the whole nine Mexican yards." She laughed heartily. "Mom Thornberry is going to help me fix it, and my momma is making pecan pie—close as I could get her to come to pralines."

That left me speechless, but fortunately Mike arrived with a hazmat guy, all suited in white protective gear, in tow. "You surely don't expect it to blow up, do you?" I asked in disbelief.

Mike was patient. "No, but we don't know what's in it. Did you touch it?"

I nodded. "I was not sure about opening it, but Keisha made me stop and put it down."

"Thanks, Keisha," he said. "I'm always glad you're here to take care of Kelly. Even if you operate on instinct." He was grinning now.

"Mike Shandy, you best be careful with me." Keisha tried to frown at him, but she smiled enough to give herself away.

The hazmat guy, who Mike introduced as Weldon, was fingering the lettering. "Where's the parking lot?" he asked. "I'll take it out there to open it, but I don't think there's anything suspicious in there." Mike showed him the way, and they disappeared but were back within minutes.

"Nothing but a threat," Mike said, holding the letter by one corner with his gloved hand.

I moved to snatch it from him. "It's mine. Let me read it."

He whirled away, with an almost ballerina-like grace. "No gloves, Kelly. I'll read it."

Weldon put a white sheet of paper on the empty desk in the office, and Mike carefully laid the letter on it, while I fidgeted with curiosity.

Finally, he read, slowly, "Ms. O'Connell, Sandra will be returned to her home and you will not be bothered if you simply refuse to accept the inheritance. Those are my terms."

"No signature," Mike said, but there is a postscript. "You're not going to like this, Kelly."

"I already don't like it."

"It says, 'I noticed how attractive your older daughter is. I know you want her to be safe.'"

For a moment I thought I'd faint. Keisha was quicker than Mike and was at my side instantly, her strong arms easing me back into my chair. My breath was coming in great gulps, and my whole body shook.

Mike crossed the room in one great stride and instead of hugging me, did the unexpected—he slapped my face sharply. "Kelly, get a grip. This is simply meant to scare you. Don't let it do that."

I began to babble. "I don't want that money. Never did. Tell him he can have it. Just let Sandra go and leave us alone. Oh, what if he took Maggie. I...I couldn't bear it, Mike. You've got to do something."

His hands were now steady on my shoulders. "Come on, Kelly. You know that's not the solution. He's kidnapped someone, threatened you, committed more than one act of vandalism. We don't just lie down and say, 'Have it your way.' At least I as a police officer don't, and I don't expect you to either. I promise," and he looked me straight in the eyes, "I will keep Maggie safe."

I sat frozen like a stone, horror holding me in its grasp.

Mike turned to Weldon. "Take that downtown for analysis, would you? And thanks. Tell them I want a copy of it as soon as possible."

Keisha was like the calm voice of practicality. "You can't trace a typewriter like that, can you? Must be older than God."

Mike seemed glad to fix his mind on details. "We might trace it if we ever found a machine that old, but that's like looking for a needle in a haystack. I have no idea where to begin. The postmark was Waco."

Neither Keisha nor I had noticed that. "Waco?" I echoed.

"If I was going to send a threat like that, I sure wouldn't use a post office anywhere near Fort Worth," Mike said. "This guy is cunning. And that scares me."

I wished he hadn't said that. It was only eleven thirty but suddenly I was in a yank to get Maggie, right away! The girls' schools were both to be dismissed at noon that day. I asked Keisha to get Em and said I was heading for the middle school.

Mike watched me, bit his tongue—I saw him do it—and kissed me. "She'll be fine, sweetheart. Let's not let this ruin Christmas."

No, but I'm keeping her by me every minute.

Obsessed, I was ten minutes early to get Maggie. She was used to having to wait for me, and she knows me too well. When she saw me sitting in the car, at the very head of the line of waiting parents, she did a bit of panic herself.

"Mom? What's wrong? Why are you here so early?" She threw herself and her backpack into the car and looked at me anxiously.

I tried to be casual. "Nothing's wrong, Mag. Calm down. I just decided Keisha could get Em and I'd get you and we'll have a celebration lunch. It is the last day of school before Christmas vacation."

"Well, of course I know that." Her voice had that "duh" tone in it, so typical of teenagers.

"Where do you want to go to lunch?"

"Bun Appetit," she replied without hesitation.

So I asked her to use my phone to call Keisha—number two on speed dial of course—and tell her to meet us, with Em, at Mona's hot dog stand.

We had hot dogs and root beer floats (shades of my childhood) and a wonderful, giggly time in anticipation of Christmas, though I never thought I would giggle again. It was way too cold to eat outside, so I was somewhat more at ease with the girls inside with me, and I was able, briefly, to put Greg Davis out of my mind. I wished Keisha would stop giving me sideways looks every so often.

****

That night, when the girls were sleep, Mike told me he was going to Gatesville on Monday. This was only Thursday, and Christmas was Saturday, so we'd be past the holiday. But it still seemed awfully soon to me. "Monday?"

"I think I've known for some time I'd have to go talk to Jo Ellen, and now that we know it's the inheritance behind all this, I have no choice. I'll call down there tomorrow. Are you working?"

"No. I closed the office." I didn't add that I was going to stay home and keep both girls with me, preferably in the same room.

"Okay. I'll be off early, and we can have a quiet family Christmas Eve at your mom's."

I nodded but said, "I wish we could stay home. I don't want

Maggie out of this house at all, and I feel safer here. But I don't want to tell Mom about the threats." I honestly thought I was going to cry.

"I'll talk to Cynthia," he said and left the room, cell phone in hand. Pretty soon, he returned. "I explained that girls wanted Christmas Eve at home and really didn't want that oyster stew you told me about. She seemed okay with that, but when I asked if she and Otto would join us here, she said they were looking forward to oyster stew. They're coming for dessert, and she's bringing old-fashioned plum pudding—already made. Even has the hard sauce."

"Mike, did I ever tell you I love you?"

"Tell me again. Then I'm going shopping."

He brought home a beef tenderloin that he roasted to a perfect medium rare. We had oven-roasted rosemary potatoes and fresh spinach (which the girls had recently learned to love). Sparkling grape juice for the girls, Perrier for me, red wine for Mike. Cynthia and Otto arrived about eight with plum pudding which to my surprise, the girls liked. It had been liberally soaked in bourbon, and I think the girls liked the hard sauce as much as the pudding. I could barely finish one small slice. An elegant meal with no mention of any troubles looming over us. They didn't stay long, and we all hugged and kissed as they left and said we'd see them tomorrow at Claire's.

In spite of their sophisticated knowledge that Santa didn't exist, the girls made a great show of hanging their stockings and putting out cookies, milk, and a note for Santa.

It was a perfect evening, and I basked in the glow of the wonder of my life…until Mike and I went upstairs and were getting ready for bed. As I brushed my teeth and couldn't really talk, he said, "I called the prison at Gatesville today."

I managed a mumbled "Ummm."

"Jo Ellen had a complete meltdown two days ago. Really went off her rocker, throwing things, threatening, cursing. Not the model prisoner they knew. But the Jo Ellen we knew. The warden was completely baffled, until I said we'd seen that behavior before. They're transferring Jo Ellen North to the psychiatric unit at Vernon next week. Promised to hold her through Monday so I can talk to her though I don't know which is closer, Gatesville or Vernon. Might be a close tie. Anyway I'll go to Gatesville early Monday."

I spit out my toothpaste and turned on him. "Psychiatric unit? She's no more psycho than you and I are. But she's cunning. She's conned them."

He was calm. "I thought of that, and I think you're probably right. She may well be doing whatever she's doing to avoid further prosecution if this scheme of hers goes wrong."

"You think it's her scheme? How can she do that?"

"A hundred ways, but offhand I'd say someone on the inside is giving her access to disposable cell phones. So she plots with this Greg Davis, but the calls can't be traced. And as far as prison authorities know, she has no contact with the outside world."

I simply sputtered. How could this happen? What was wrong with our prison system that she could get away with this and then convince people she was psycho? Okay, I thought she was psycho all the time, but...and then I stopped.

"What happens if she's sent to a psychiatric facility?" I asked. "Can she still inherit if I bow out?"

"I'm not sure of the law, Kelly, but I think by terms of the will the money goes into a trust same as it would now. Martin may well have stipulated that in the revised will. But she could probably have a miraculous recovery. I think she's doing whatever she's doing through this Greg guy partly out of greed and partly out of revenge. I'm sure she thinks you've ruined her life."

There's no sense in arguing when logic doesn't apply, and it did me no good to suggest she ruined her own life when she killed my ex-husband and tried to kill me.

Mike pulled me down onto the bed. "Let's make a pact not to talk about Jo Ellen or Greg Davis or any of it until Monday when I go to Gatesville. When I come home, I'll tell you everything. Meantime, Merry Christmas."

What else could a girl do except sink into his arms?

****

Christmas was a lot more fun than I anticipated, though I still always felt in the back of my mind that I was anticipating, jumping bridges that weren't there yet. We had a quiet gift exchange. The girls got the things girls that age want—a guitar for Maggie, a drafting table for Em, clothes, books, and iTunes certificates, though I hate giving gift cards. I like to pick things out personally. Mike watched in amusement as I unwrapped a cookbook that promised to tell me how to cook 365 simple and quick meals—was that a hint? And then a lovely silk scarf—except he knows I just can't do scarves. They look terrific on other women, silly on me. But then, slyly, he brought out a small box. It held a simple diamond drop necklace set in white gold that curved around the stone in a sensuous design. Perfect for me since I wore little jewelry and all of it plain. I don't go in for fancy, but I don't think I've ever had anything this perfect and lovely. I gave him a rare book on Fort Worth history that I'd found at a library sale and a smashing shirt and tie combination, if I do say so.

When everyone thought we were through with presents, I pretended to just notice a card on the tree. Mike got up to retrieve it, saw his name on it, and gave me a quizzical look. Then he opened it, read for a minute and then literally jumped in the air, yelling "Yahoo!" Of course the girls demanded to know what was in it, and he showed them: "Your newest daughter will arrive in May."

We had a group hug, with Em demanding, "What's her name?"

"Not yet," I said. "We've a long time to decide." Actually, I was thinking Claire Elisabeth sounded good.

"I suppose we can't call her Keisha the second," Em said, while Maggie hooted.

Even Mike laughed. "Nope, sweetie, Keisha is one of a kind."

Christmas dinner was a happy event, and as I looked around I realized most of my extended family didn't know what was going on in our lives—they'd read about the missing girl and shaken their heads in sadness, but they didn't know it had anything to do with us. Keisha and José of course knew the whole story, and Claire knew just a bit. But Anthony and his boys didn't, nor did his daughter Theresa and her husband Joe, nor Mona and Jenny, although I suspected Maggie had told Jenny the whole story. I wondered if she'd told Mona. If so, Mona showed no sign. They'd certainly had enough trauma in their lives, they didn't need any more. My mom was so occupied with Otto and his needs—a beer, a stool for his feet, some more of that marvelous pâté—that she was oblivious to everything else. I caught Claire glancing at me every once in a while, so I ratcheted up my happy act. A glass of wine would have helped, but I couldn't do that.

As if to join the party, the baby in my belly made her presence known by kicking, those gentle, butterfly-like feelings, not the strong kicks that would soon follow. I would have pulled Mike aside in privacy so he could feel, but I knew the kicks weren't strong enough. Still that buoyed me through the long dinner hour.

The big event of the evening was Keisha's announcement of their stepped-up wedding date. "Y'all be getting an invitation, so read your email."

I saw my mom frown in disapproval at that and poke Otto until he nodded in agreement.

"And I'll have an assignment for every one of you," Keisha went on. "This is going to be the wildest wedding you ever saw."

Everyone cried, "Where?" but they were silenced when she replied, "The Grill." Mom frowned again, and José blushed—you could see the red creep slowly across his tan face.

And then, almost anticlimactically, Christmas was over. We all helped Claire clear and clean until she finally shoved us out the door, nearly screaming that she wanted to be left in peace and quiet to do the dishes. I knew Megan and Liz would help her, so I didn't feel too badly about leaving.

Once home, we were at loose ends, a feeling I often have after a big holiday. But this time other thoughts kept creeping in. Monday, Mike would go to see Jo Ellen North. And Greg Davis had left us alone—but why, when Christmas was a perfect time to harass someone by ruining the holiday? Had he some major surprise in mind next? I looked at Maggie, absorbed in one of her Christmas books, and fear clutched at my heart.

And then I thought of the Balcombs and could only imagine how their Christmas had been. It was too late to call, and somehow a sympathy call on Christmas night didn't seem appropriate. Or maybe that was when they most needed support. I'd go see them tomorrow.

Maybe the best part of the whole day came late that night. Mike was propped up in bed reading, and I was lying next to him, my mind full of thoughts of the day and of the week to come and the problems and uncertainty it would bring.

"Mike," I said softly, "The baby kicked me today."

"She did?" He sat straight up in bed and threw his book on the bedside table. "Can I feel it?"

"No movement now, and it wasn't strong enough for you to tell or I'd have pulled you into a bathroom, no matter what people thought we were doing in there."

He laughed aloud. "That's really exciting. I mean, it makes it seem real. Knowing there's a real, moving life in there is good, Kelly."

"Yeah, if Greg Davis doesn't ruin it."

"Kelly, I love you," he said, reaching down to give me a gentle kiss. "I won't let anything happen to any of you."

"And you're going off to fight a dragon on my behalf Monday."

He gave me a wry look. "Well, sort of. Be glad the weather is okay. I can make it down and back in time for supper easily."

So then I had to plan supper.

Chapter Thirteen

Sunday afternoon about two I called the Balcombs to ask if it would be convenient for me to visit. I know at Christmas most people have more leftovers than they know what to do with, but I wanted to take them something. Leftover turkey that I'd brought home from Claire's didn't seem quite right, so I took the half a cheeseball in the fridge, re-shaped it, rolled it in fresh parsley and pecan bits, and wrapped it in red cellophane with a red ribbon, chose a small basket from my humongous collection, and tucked in an unopened pack of rice crackers. I've found it smart to keep such things on hand.

Alma Balcomb sounded tentative. "I don't know. It's been a hard week for us."

"I'm sure," I said, "but I just want to come give you a hug. I've thought about you so much all weekend."

"That's kind of you. Yes, come ahead. I'll tell Janice and Joe you're on your way."

On impulse, I tucked a bottle of nice pinot grigio in the basket, told Mike and the girls where I was going, and left. I parked in front of the Balcombs and walked up the sidewalk but this time I didn't see the curtain move. Just before I rang that chime-like doorbell, I paused because I heard loud voices coming from inside.

"Mom, you must *not* tell her." Janice sounded frantic, furious.

"Young lady," Joe Balcomb said, "you will not tell us what to do. We're all in this together, scared to death about your sister, and we will do what we think best."

I decided it was time to ring the bell. It took a few minutes for them to answer. My guess was that they were collecting themselves. And when I was courteously shown in, I was aware that Janice had fled the room.

I offered my gift, saying that it was just a token, but I hoped they'd enjoy it.

"So thoughtful of you," Alma said. "I know we will, though we're not drinking people."

Joe grabbed the bottle and said, "You may not be, Alma, but right about now I need a drink. Ms. O'Connell, will you join me?"

I shook my head. "Please, call me Kelly. But no, I can't join you. I'm expecting."

They both brightened a bit at this news, and Alma hugged me. "I'm so happy for you. You have two children, don't you?"

Why did I feel a little dread when I answered yes?

Alma said, "Joe, I believe I'll have just a bit of wine, and pour some for Janice. I'll ask her to put this cheese and crackers on a plate. Kelly, what can I get you to drink?"

I asked for water, and pretty soon we were having a sort of mid-afternoon happy hour. Janice joined us, but she looked far from happy. In fact, she glowered at her mom.

"How was Christmas?" I ventured.

"Pretty sad," Alma admitted. "We sort of went through the motions. Neighbors did invite us for dinner, but Janice refused to go...."

"I didn't feel like being sociable," the girl said. "Mom, enough."

But Alma wasn't to be stopped. "It was a good thing she stayed home because about five Sandra called."

My hand shook when I put the water glass down, and it was an effort to keep my voice controlled as I said, "What a relief to know she's alive."

Alma looked startled. "We never doubted that. Did you?"

I stared at her in amazement. Of course I doubted it. I feared for weeks, for it had been that long now, that Mike would come home with the report of a body found in a wooded field somewhere remote. Each night I said a prayer of gratitude that hadn't happened. How could the Balcombs be so naïve? But I remember other cases where families held out hope when there was none—in rare instances their faith was justified, but in most cases that strongly held belief only made them more vulnerable when bad news came.

And why in heaven's name hadn't they called Mike?

I turned to Janice. "What did she say? Is she all right?"

Janice shrugged and avoided looking at me. "She says she's all right. She wants to come home, but they won't let her."

My mind fixed on the word "they." We thought, assumed, it was Greg Davis holding her. But "they" indicated more than one person. I knew I should call Mike right away, but then I'd have to go home to be with the girls, so he could question the Balcombs. I pushed on. "Did she say where she was or who 'they' were?"

Janice still looked resentful. "No. Someone was right there, listening to what she said. She just said she wanted us to know she was being treated well and in no danger. Then someone grabbed the phone and cut off the call."

"Why didn't you call the police? Specifically my husband?"

"She asked me not to. Said that would put her in danger. I suppose now you're going to tell." The hostility and anger in her voice and in her eyes were almost too much to bear.

"No, I'm going to let you do that. But, yes, I have to tell him." I said my goodbyes to Joe and Alma, with a hug for the latter, and said I was sure Mike would be in touch that day. And then I was out the door— and speeding home to run breathlessly inside.

Mike looked up from the jigsaw puzzle he and Em were doing. "What's the rush, Kelly?"

"Mike, the Balcombs heard from Sandra yesterday. You've got to talk to them."

He wasn't in as big as rush as I was. "That's good. At least she's alive. What did she say?"

I spilled out the story, sure that he'd jump up from the table and rush over to the Balcombs' house. Instead, he said, "Look, Em. This one goes there and it completes that face."

She clapped her hands.

"Em, I've got to go. You can keep working or you can wait until I get back." He pulled out his phone, called someone and asked for a trace on a call to the Balcombs' about five last night. "Probably a disposable phone but they can give me a general idea of the area where the call came from. I'll go on over there, but I doubt I'll learn much more than you did." He put an arm around my shoulders. "Kelly, once more, you're jumping into my work."

"I didn't mean to," I said indignantly. "I went over there to make a compassionate call. This just happened."

He raised an eyebrow at me as he got his jacket. I noticed he reached up on the high shelf for his service revolver and put it in his pocket.

"You going to call for someone to meet you there?"

He raised an eyebrow. "Do you really think I need backup?"

I wanted to ask if he didn't why he'd put his gun in his pocket, but instead I sat down and started to work on Em's puzzle, a complicated thousand-piece thing on Santa's workshop.

Mike was gone about two hours, home in time for turkey soup for supper, and unusually silent about his mission. The girls ate in silence too, though Maggie commented that she was glad 'that missing girl' was alive. Then she said she and Jenny thought they might go to the mall since there was no school tomorrow and Mona said she'd drive and pick them up.

"No!" My voice came out louder and more strident than I'd meant.

Mike raised that blasted eyebrow at me again.

"Mom, you've let us do that before. What's wrong now?"

Mike rescued me. "Maggie, you know someone's threatening your mom, right?"

She nodded.

"That threat may extend to you girls, and we want to keep you safe until this is over. I have a feeling it won't be long. Can you help us?"

Maggie pushed her soup bowl away. "Yeah, I guess. But it's gonna be a long week of vacation. What'll we do?"

My idea came bubbling out of my mouth. "Why not ask Keisha to take you girls? She wants to shop for a wedding dress and lingerie and all those kinds of things. She keeps saying she'll shop online, but I bet she'd love a trip to the mall."

Em's eyes lit up. "Can I go too then?"

I looked at Maggie, who said, "I guess so, squirt, if you won't be a pain."

Em looked hurt. "I'm never a pain."

Maggie just looked at her.

After dinner, I called Keisha, who was delighted with the idea. "Mona can go too, and we'll go early enough that José can escort us. Course he can't see my gown." Then she hesitated. "You be all right in the office alone?"

I assured her I would, and we agreed that the girls would stay with Mona until ten o'clock in the morning, when Keisha and José would pick them up, take them to the mall, and even buy them lunch at one of those awful food court places.

Late that night, Mike told me he didn't get much more out of the Balcombs than I had—more than one person, apparently safe quarters, no obvious distress. "I don't think the parents know any more, but the sister does. She's hiding something. I think maybe she hears from Sandra more than she lets on and only told her folks yesterday because it was Christmas. Sort of like a Christmas present."

"But if she knows more, why would she hide it?" I asked.

"I think someone's threatening her—either with her sister's safety or her own. But she's one scared puppy."

"Can you trace the call? "

"Phone company says disposable cell phone, made from somewhere on the west side of the city. And he's smart. Turns it off when he's not using it."

"Leaves a lot of territory," said.

"Yeah. I asked them to put a bug on the Balcombs' phone—with their permission of course. And one on our land line, now that we have one. Not that it will do much good. He seems to have your cell number. We may have to bug that too."

I bit off a comment about asking my permission—sometimes I was just too prickly for my own good. Thinking of his trip the next day, I asked how this connected to Jo Ellen North. He put his head in his hands and said, "No way that I can see. That's puzzling me, and believe me, I've been thinking about it."

As he turned over to go to sleep, Mike said drowsily, "Kelly, take your gun to work tomorrow."

"I already promised Keisha." But his request sent a chill through me. He was nervous about me in the office alone, and if he was, so was I.

****

The next morning, I saw Mike off at six-thirty—I protested he didn't have to leave that early, and he simply said the earlier he left the sooner he'd be back. I wished he weren't going, but that wasn't my call. Jo Ellen would stonewall him that much I knew. But he would have to see for himself. Mike was darn good at sizing people up, so who knows what he'd discover.

I wakened the girls, but I was so edgy I know I was cross with them. They didn't have to hurry—if I was a bit late opening the day after Christmas, I doubted the real estate market in Fairmount would collapse, and Mona would be home until at least nine-thirty, so there was no rush getting them to her. And yet I hurried them, even while scolding myself for being compulsive.

"I want, just one day this week, to sleep until I wake up," Maggie said sullenly. "Even if I wake up to an empty house."

That wasn't going to happen, but I bit my tongue and promised to see what I could do about it. Then I rushed them into the car and took them to Mona's apartment, stopping only to be sure they were inside and with Mona and Jenny. Then I got to an empty office and wondered why I was in such a hurry to get there. I made coffee and read the paper. Real estate would wait.

An uneasy feeling settled over me at the office. As I worked I kept glancing out the front windows—why had we thought an office with plate glass windows was a good idea? I felt like a sitting duck. I had my gun in my jacket pocket, my cell phone by my hand, and I still jumped at every noise. Usually I'd tell you I like solitude sometimes, but today I longed for someone, anyone—except Greg Davis—to come in to talk about houses or the neighborhood or something.

The phone rang exactly once, and when I answered it eagerly, it was Mike telling me he was pulling into the prison complex at Gatesville. Of course I was relieved that he was safely there but that had never been one of my major worries. I asked him to call when he left, and he said he would.

By eleven o'clock, I felt myself going stir-crazy, so I decided it was time to drive the neighborhood. I had three street appraisals to do, and in general I just wanted to see if there were any For Sale by Owner or For Rent signs out. Even then I was cautious, weaving in and out of one-way and dead-end streets that an outsider to the neighborhood wouldn't know and watching carefully for anyone following me. That was a bit silly because I had no idea what kind of car Greg Davis drove. I couldn't concentrate on street appraisals, and it occurred to me I should come back with Em to do them. She always had definite opinions on houses that I was considering, and she more often than not proved to be right. Of course that gave me a pang, thinking about the girls happily shopping with Keisha. Of course they were safe. I'd have heard if they weren't.

By noon I decided I was hungry and went to the Grill, where I ordered a hamburger steak, medium rare, with mashed potatoes and salad with ranch.

"You expecting Mike? Want to order for him?" Peter asked.

"Nope, just me today. Thanks, though."

I found a seat at a table in the back room and pondered. I didn't want to tell Peter that Mike was out of town because who knew who else was listening. If that wasn't paranoia, I didn't know what was. Deliberately I got out my phone and began checking Facebook, but I knew I was simply trying to keep my mind off my anxiety. I wanted Mike back in Fort Worth, Keisha back in the office, and the girls safely at home with me.

Just as my food was delivered, my phone rang. Keisha gushed, literally. "We are having the best time. And wait till you see my wedding gown. Em picked it out. It's just perfect. We're going to have lunch, shop a bit more, and then we'll be at the office by three. I got to catch up on all the details you ignored all day."

"I did *not* leave anything undone. If fact, I had a fine, productive day by myself."

"Yeah, sure. You eatin' lunch at your desk?"

"Nope. I'm at the Grill. Havin' a great meal. See you later." And I punched the off button. They'd be back in two hours or a little more, and I'd be just fine until then. I polished off every bite of my meal and headed back to the office with a renewed sense of self-confidence. I'd write up notes on the street appraisals, even though I'd been haphazard about them. As I thought about the three houses, more details came back to me, and I decided I'd bid on two of the three.

So there I was, acting brave, working on my computer, when something crashed through the front window. I jumped, screamed and looked—and then I screamed again. It was a bottle of liquid with a rag stuffed in the top. I knew enough about Molotov cocktails to go into an absolute spin. I had the sense to grab my phone, but my feet seemed leaden, not willing to listen to the brain that was telling them to move—quickly. I finally made it to the rear hallway of the building, knocked on the office next door and yelled, "Evacuate, now!" and finally found myself in the parking lot, waiting for the noise of an explosion.

Nothing happened. For five long minutes, nothing happened.

The people from the accountant's office stood around looking at me as though I'd lost my mind.

With shaking hands I dialed the district police office and reported what had happened. The order came back, "Stay clear of the premises. We'll be right there."

I relayed this advice to the people standing around me, but they looked skeptical. Still none of them went inside.

Then a new cause for panic crept into my brain. What if Keisha brought the girls back and went in the front door right now. I punched the speed dial number for Keisha's phone and asked where they were.

"Oh, honey, we're still shopping. We just bought your girls some lingerie." She chortled. "They're getting' to that age, you know."

I did not want to discuss the issue of girls and bras and age at that point. "Go to the house," I ordered. "Don't come to the office."

"Kelly, you okay?"

"Yes, I think so. Just do what I ask." And once again I ended the call.

The police arrived, compete with a Hazmat team, and one lone officer I didn't know came to talk to us. "We think it's harmless," he said. "But we'll ask you to stay outside for a little longer."

Eventually they decided it was water inside the bottle, but they tried, without success to get prints off the bottle and took it away as evidence. "You did the right thing," one of the officers told me, as though he were patting a child on the head and telling me I was a good girl.

I called Anthony, told him what had happened, and asked him to come clean up and board the window. He said, "Right quick, Miss Kelly. I be there right quick."

While I waited, I began picking up the largest pieces of glass and putting them in a cardboard box I found in a closet. Bless Keisha, she always knew everything would come in handy sometime. Then I began to sweep, dumping the dustpan of glass shards into the same large box.

Anthony was distraught when he arrived. "Miss Kelly, I do that. You don't."

"I had to keep busy," I said. "Is your shop vac in your truck to get the rest of this?"

He clapped his hand to his white hair. "No, but I get it. I finish cleaning after I board up. You go home now, Miss Kelly. You need rest. You take care of yourself and that little one."

He didn't know how right he was.

Mike called. "Kelly, what's going on up there? You okay? They called me about a bomb threat."

I explained about the faux Molotov cocktail and said Anthony was boarding up and would be back to finish cleaning and lock up. I was going home. Mike said he'd had an interesting but not productive interview with Jo Ellen and would tell me went he got home. I picked up my purse, told Anthony thanks and goodbye, ignored the flashing message light. It could wait until tomorrow or at least later tonight. I never wanted to get out of a place so fast.

As I left the building, I apologized to the accountant's staff profusely, probably too many times.

****

Poor Mike came home about six to confusion and a hungry family, including Keisha who had stayed after she returned the girls from shopping, and Claire who came for a glass of wine on her way home and stayed to hear the story. There wasn't much to tell Mike that he didn't already know—someone had thrown a fake Molotov cocktail through my office window, scared the living daylights out of me, and thoroughly smashed the window.

"Next time," I said, "we're getting shatterproof glass. What if someone had been sitting close to that window?"

"Like me," Keisha chimed in. "My desk is up front and personal to that door…and that window."

I hadn't even thought of that. "We better check your desk for glass in the morning. Sorry. I took my frustration out sweeping the floor and picking up the largest pieces of glass."

She shrugged.

"I herded the whole building—the accountant and all his staff—out into the parking lot and then felt foolish. I guess the phone rang while we were out there because the message light flashed but I never did listen. I just didn't care."

Mike picked up my cell phone, handed it to me, and said, "Call right now and listen to that message but don't erase it."

I dialed obediently, knowing I should have done that earlier. When I heard the message, such a chill went through me that I visibly shuddered and handed the phone to Mike. He listened intently, pressed two to save, and looked at all of us.

"Essentially it was a double threat—next time the Molotov cocktail will be real and he knows the girls, particularly Maggie, were at the mall today."

"How can a fugitive be so many places?" I asked. "And for goodness sake, how would he know to follow the girls to the mall?"

"It's more than one person," Mike said with certainty. "Has to be. And I guess Greg Davis has changed his appearance again—dramatically. Or he wouldn't be walking the streets. My guess is he threw the cocktail, so who was at the mall?"

Em sidled up to me and held tight, her thin body quivering. I soothed her hair with one hand and whispered, "Mike won't let anything happen to any of us." She just closed her eyes.

Maggie sat on the couch, or rather slouched, arms across her chest in a belligerent pose. "I suppose now I can't go anywhere, even with Keisha." Anger glittered in her eyes.

Mike sat down next to her. "Maggie, would you rather be careful and safe for a little while, so you can do all the things girls in high school do. This won't go on forever. I give you my word."

She looked at him without comment, though I thought her body relaxed a little. Finally, she muttered, "I guess so," and got up to go to her room. No doubt to call Jenny.

Mike's next order of business was practical. He sent Claire to the new Italian restaurant to get spaghetti, meatballs, and salad for all of us. While she was gone, he opened a bottle of red wine to share with Claire, poured kid wine for Em and me, and offered Keisha beer.

"Naw," she said, "with spaghetti, I think I'll join you for the red wine."

The thought of food turned my stomach. "I can't eat."

Keisha calmly said, "You'll eat if I have to spoon feed you."

And that's practically what happened, though I found I was hungrier than I thought. Mike knew what he was doing—we all needed food so we could think clearly. I picked at my dinner, with an occasional nudge from Keisha, but the others ate heartily. Claire and Keisha cleared the dishes, recycling what they could, and stored leftovers in the fridge, while Mike made small talk with the girls about what they'd seen at the mall. I knew he didn't want to talk about his visit with Jo Ellen, and since nobody knew where he'd been, it didn't come up. Much as I longed to find out all about it, I kept quiet.

Talk turned to Keisha's wedding, and even Maggie got her enthusiasm back about the wedding dress, which roused my curiosity. But all three of them remained mum on the details, though the girls trotted out their bridesmaids gowns. I gasped. Keisha had said Em's dress would be pink but I wasn't expecting the yards of almost fluorescent pink that encased my youngest child. As she twirled, the dress moved around her with a life of its own. The neckline was sufficiently demure, but oh, the color!

Then Maggie appeared wearing equally bright turquoise but totally different in style—almost severe, a miniskirt on a dress that clung to her slim body. I wanted to cry out "No!" because that dress, more than anything else, made me realize Maggie was turning from girl to young lady.

Keisha stood silently watching my reaction, and I'm sure my

thought flashed visibly across my face. "You like them?" she finally asked. "I gave them color guidelines and said they could each pick their own dress." Then a bit defensively, she added, "Bridesmaids' dresses don't have to match each other."

Claire chimed in before I could say something tactless. "They certainly don't. Having everything match is a bit passé these days. Why, even your dining chairs don't have to match."

Almost inadvertently I turned my head to the perfectly matched oak dining table and chairs Mrs. Hunt had left in the house. At the same time, Keisha said, "Mine don't. But then I only have three. That's why we don't entertain." And she laughed heartily at her own joke.

The best I could do was to say, "I'm speechless. They…they're not what I would have chosen."

"Me either," Keisha said, "though I like them. These dresses are who they are."

I glanced at Mike, but he just reached out and squeezed my hand. I looked at my two girls, standing side by side, one still young and trusting, the other rapidly moving into the teen years and cynicism and a bit of independence—well, more than a bit. No wonder she thought my troubles hemmed her in. My heart really went out to Maggie. Greg Davis was complicating an important time in her life…and so was I.

"Okay," I said, my voice once again strong and cheerful. "Trot out the wedding dress."

Keisha shook her head. "Nope, that's a surprise. And it's not even here. We took it to my momma's so José wouldn't see it. You'll see it January twenty-sixth and not before."

I tried imagining. Would she wear white, even though a tad inappropriate? Surely not a muumuu or a tunic with pants, though I knew who would wear the pants in that marriage. Finally I settled on an image I could see in my mind—Keisha swathed in yards of white gauze over satin, studied with rhinestone beads. The effect was entirely different from Em's gauzy dress. What bridal gallery carried such a gown, in a size to fit Keisha? I had too much on my mind to spend more time worrying about it.

Gradually our guests left for home, still shaking and mumbling over the explosion at my office. The wedding talk and fashion show hadn't really distracted them.

Chapter Fourteen

Maggie went into her room and closed the door, but Em announced she was sleeping with us. "I'll bring a pallet."

Mike pulled her onto his lap, though she was getting a bit gangly and ungainly for lap sitting. "Em, that's fine. But would you go read or watch TV with Maggie, so your mom and I can have some private time."

She looked a little skeptical. Probably she suspected private time would mean talk about something she wanted to hear. But Em was a trooper, "If it's okay with Mag. You go ask her."

Mike knocked and stuck his head in Maggie's room. The words I heard sounded less like a request than a strong suggestion, but Maggie apparently agreed, and Em grabbed a book—"I don't always like her TV programs"—and marched into the room, carefully closing the door behind her.

Once we were upstairs, Mike kicked off his shoes and threw himself on the bed, lying on his back, hands behind his head, staring at the ceiling. I sat on the edge of the bed beside him.

"Well?"

He knew exactly what I meant. "She's crazy. Bat-shit crazy. What scares me is that her one mission in life is to hurt you, even kill you."

That surprised me, even as much as I knew about Jo Ellen. For someone to have no purpose in life except my death was an immense and scary thought. "Kill me?" People had wanted to kill me before, but it was never as deliberate as this sounded. "She can't kill me if she's locked up, can she?"

"She's pulling the strings for whatever's going on here. What I can't figure is this transfer to the state mental prison at Vernon. She's got the authorities in Gatesville convinced she's gone over the edge, and I believed it myself today. Remember how difficult she was to control when she was arrested? Kept threatening the cops, fought like a tiger. And in the courtroom, where the judge finally had her shackled and gagged. Today was worse if possible—foul language, frightening images of what she'd like to do to you, threats that she had friends on the outside."

"I thought you said she had no visitors, no mail, no communication with the outside world."

He sighed. "Once again, I was wrong as I suspected all along. The warden and I talked it over. She's apparently using someone else at the prison to convey her messages. We're not sure if she asks them to tell visitors or she uses their cell phones. Inmates aren't supposed to have phones, but in a population like that, some get away with it. Jo Ellen has enough discretionary cash to do some pretty impressive bribery."

I shook my head to clear the cobwebs. "But if she's crazy enough to be institutionalized how can she be doing that?"

Mike looked straight at me. "I'm no psychologist, but Jo Ellen has always had that uncontrollable temper, and I think she's learned to put it to her own good, or bad, use. So now she's using it to go from Gatesville to Vernon. Almost the same distance from Fort Worth and she loses her contacts, cohorts, whatever at Gatesville. Maybe, though, she thinks security is less tight there. Somehow she thinks it works to her advantage."

"But aren't the criminally insane locked up securely?"

"Supposed to be. But you were right days ago when you said she's crazy like a fox."

"When does she go to Vernon?"

"End of the week. I'm going to call and make contact with the warden up there, ask for reports on visitors, all that stuff. I've no idea how much good it will do." He stared at the ceiling again. "Meantime, if Greg Davis threw that fake bomb this afternoon, who saw Maggie at the mall? Threats to Maggie take this to a whole different level. I can't arm a thirteen-year-old girl. And only a scumbag threatens a child. How low can you sink?"

A thought had been flitting around in the back of my mind. "Sandra? Maybe she's a willing accomplice, not a kidnap victim. But why would she put her family through that misery?"

Mike sat straight up. "Kelly, you may be right. She doesn't want her family to know how…what's the word? Misguided she's become…."

I almost laughed. "If it's true, misguided is a mild term."

"But she sees a reward, either monetary or the love of this Greg Davis, though why she'd want him I can't imagine. Or both."

"Where do we go from here?"

"We don't, Kelly. I do, as a police officer. Remember, criminal investigator and humanitarian. We're separating them and sharing different responsibilities. You keep in touch with the Balcombs. You may just have hit on what Janice Balcomb knows and is so terrified we'll find out."

I wasn't happy but I'd agreed to this bargain.

Both girls were sound asleep in Maggie's room, Mag in her bed and Em on her pallet. I voted we leave them, and we did. But in the wee hours, Em padded upstairs, Gus at her heels, and said, "I told you guys I needed to sleep up here tonight."

We simply moved over and made room for her.

My dreams that night were of prison bars and Jo Ellen shaking them and screaming obscenities, shopping malls and someone following Maggie, and Alma and Joe Balcomb on their knees in front of me begging, while Greg Davis laughed in the background.

****

Already mid-January, the girls were back in school after what seemed an endless, boring vacation, and it was time for my monthly check-up with Mrs. Buxton in Dr. Goodwin's office. To my surprise, this time I saw the doctor herself.

"Mrs. Buxton is not feeling well today."

I expressed my regrets and said how solicitous she always was, how concerned about my general health and any stress I was feeling. I wasn't going to tell even Sherrie Goodwin about the stress in my life.

"Are you stressed?" Sherrie Goodwin asked.

"Not really," I said. "Just the usual stresses of balancing work and family life and trying to figure out a problem with an inheritance settlement."

She laughed. "I'm sure the latter can be stressful."

I wanted to say not nearly as stressful as knowing there's a professional hit man out there with a high-powered rifle and a bull's eye on my back.

"How are you feeling?" she asked, flipping through the chart.

"Fine," I said. "No morning sickness, good appetite. I've been eating fairly healthily"—maybe a stretch on my part.

"Exercising?"

"Not as much as I should," I confessed. "Always too busy."

She frowned. "Mrs. Buxton's notes record a high level of stress. Also high blood pressure…we don't want you going into pre-eclampsia. You peeing a lot?"

"No more than usual for a pregnant woman," I said. After all, I'd had experience with this.

She took my blood pressure to confirm the reading the nurse had found. "118/70. I wouldn't call that high." She went back to flipping through the charts. "Funny, every time you've come in, the nurse assistant has found normal range, but then Mrs. Buxton confirmed she got a high rating, as high as 145/105, which is dangerous. I wonder why she didn't bring this to my attention before." She checked my lungs, listened to the baby's heart rate, all the usual things. Then she said, "Sit here a few minutes—are you in a rush?"

I shook my head.

"Usually if a patient has high blood pressure, it's when she comes in—nerves about a doctor appointment, rushing to get here, that kind of thing. Your pattern is just the opposite. Let me come back in after my next patient and check it again." And she was gone.

Luckily I had my cell phone, so I called Keisha, told her I'd be delayed at the doctor's office, and pondered the puzzle of Mrs. Buxton and my high blood pressure. When I took it at home, it was normal; Dr. Goodwin always got normal. I had no way to check what Mrs. Buxton saw, so was she bluffing? Trying to scare me? Another of the scare tactics that seemed to be all around me? My earlier suspicion about the techniques of stalking surfaced again—this might just be a new form of rattling my cage. But why Mrs. Buxton?

Dr. Goodwin came in, took my blood pressure again and reported 120/70. Laughing, she said, "I suppose it went up two points because I gave you something to worry about. You're just fine, Kelly, but let me give you the name of a yoga studio that has classes for moms-to-be. Gentle workout and yet it will get you stretching, moving those muscles, getting ready for childbirth. Also if you could walk, even ten minutes a day, that would be helpful."

I didn't want to explain why Mike didn't want me walking alone, but maybe he'd go with me evenings when he could—and when January and February didn't hit too hard. I thanked Sherrie Goodwin—should I call her Sherrie or Dr. Goodwin?—and said I hoped Mrs. Buxton would be fine soon and return to work.

"I do too," she said ruefully. "She's been a great help to me, and I can't tell you how I miss her when she's out."

Without even thinking, I asked, "So this isn't the first time she's been out?"

She threw her hands in the air. "Lord no! Almost more often than not the last several weeks. And yet, I'm reluctant to let her go. Invaluable employees like her are hard to find."

I thought of Keisha and mumbled, "I know." Then I asked, "How were you fortunate enough to find her?"

"I listed an opening with a professional agency, and she came highly recommended. She'd worked for a home care service, caring for an elderly gentleman with no family. He was highly pleased, but when he died, she said she'd gotten too attached to him. Didn't want that kind of one-on-one relationship anymore." Sherrie ran her hand through her hair. "She'd be perfect if her attendance hadn't gotten so irregular."

"It wasn't always?"

"Nope. Started, oh, about Thanksgiving." She rose, and I knew she had to get back to other patients.

I thanked her, made my next appointment, and left the office. Mrs. Buxton stayed in my thoughts, especially her irregular absences, which began about the time Sandra Balcomb disappeared. I wondered, way in the back of my mind, if Sandra Balcomb kept her from work. The next time I went to the Balcombs, I'd make it a point to ask Janice what she knew.

I went back to the office where Keisha was still waiting for details of Mike's visit with Jo Ellen at Gatesville. "Not good," I said.

"What did you expect?" Keisha asked. "She's sly, that one."

It occurred to me to wonder if Jo Ellen, being in a mental hospital, could contest a will in court. Would she be considered competent? I decided to call Benjamin Cruze.

"Hi, Benjamin," I said when his assistant finally put the call through. "I would not want you to think I'm anxious for my money or anything like that."

"I wouldn't blame you if you were. I know I could do a lot for my family with that money," he said with a laugh. But it was a forced laugh.

"I'm not quite as removed from this case as you may think. I'm pretty sure I know who's contesting the will, and I know she's going to be in a mental hospital. Is she still judged capable of bringing suit?"

I could hear caution in the silence. Finally, he said, "I don't know how you know that, and I don't particularly want to know. But the person you inquired about has appointed a surrogate to represent her."

"Can you tell me his or her name?"

A long sigh came over the phone. "Charles Sanford."

The pieces of the puzzle were beginning to come together, though they still didn't make sense. It was like finding a piece that you knew belonged to the white horse in the western jigsaw puzzle but you didn't know where to put it. Was it the nose or the tail?

I thought quickly. "Have you met him?"

"No, we have an appointment this afternoon."

"Would you do me the favor of describing him after that?"

"I suppose so. Kelly, you're not going to appear in court, are you?" His voice sounded plaintive.

"No, Benjamin, but if Charles Sanford is who I think he is, he won't be in court either."

****

Benjamin Cruze called me at home late that afternoon, while I was fixing supper. "I met Charles Sanford this afternoon," he said. "Seems like an upstanding, forthright guy."

"What does he look like?" My question was almost a demand.

"Late forties, thinning hair, beginning to go gray. Do you know him?"

No way was this the man who pulled a knife on me. Unless he had an awfully good makeup artist. "And on behalf of the person he's representing, he's contesting the will?"

Benjamin hesitated. "Yes. On grounds that Mr. Martin wasn't in his right mind when he made out the last will, eliminating a large portion of the…other person's share…who had previously been the principal beneficiary."

Why are we pussyfooting around here? Why can't we just say that Robert Martin disowned his daughter, Jo Ellen North, after she killed my ex-husband and tried to kill me? And after he learned his wife had killed his pregnant lover and Jo Ellen, as a child, had witnessed that and kept it secret all these years.

"So now what happens?" I asked.

"A probate court will hear the case. I imagine Mr. Sanford will appear."

"Let me know the date and time, please, Benjamin. I intend to appear after all. With my lawyer." Terrell Johnson had no idea what I was about to get him into. I fleetingly thought I better invite him to dinner and give him the backstory.

"Are you sure?" Benjamin asked. "I thought you weren't all that interested in the money."

"I am now," I said. "Jo Ellen North nearly killed me, and she killed my ex-husband. And I see no reason to back off now."

That left him speechless for a few moments, and then he managed, "I'll get back to you."

With a brusque "Thanks," I hung up the phone. And then I sat and pondered. Why did I want that money so badly? Mike and I made enough between us to keep our family comfortable. I didn't think the new baby would add that much financial strain. Still, half of Robert Martin's estate would probably buy a lot of diapers and baby clothes and all those cute things I hadn't been able to buy the girls…and still leave a hefty chunk for college funds. But we would be just fine without it. So why was I willing to fight?

I didn't want to think of myself as a vengeful person, and yet maybe that was it. Jo Ellen North had done some awful things to me—did I want revenge? I didn't like that idea and pushed it away. Did I think Robert Martin owed me something? Surely not. All I'd done was put his daughter in jail and push his wife over to the far edge of senility.

It occurred to me that maybe the Lord wanted me to have that money to pay it forward. Maybe I should put some away for the children's college and give the rest to the Edna Gladney Adoption Agency—after all, that was where Sheila had been born and it was an agency that could have helped Marie Winton when she found herself pregnant with Robert Martin's child, not that she wanted help or knew she needed it. But I was afraid to attribute my determination to such altruistic emotions.

I picked up the phone and called Terrell Johnson.

When he was on the line—I loved that he answered his own phone—I asked if he was busy for supper the next night. Instead of saying yea or nay, he asked, "What's up, Kelly? Not that I don't enjoy dinner at your house, but there's usually something you haven't told me."

"I need your professional services, and I'll pay your going rate. I want to explain it to you, with Mike present."

"As always you have me curious…but, let's see. Ms. Lorna is out of the picture, unfortunately. What else can it be?"

"Just be at the house at six," I said. "No big surprise this time, but I'll need your expertise in probate court."

"I'm no probate expert," he stammered.

"You'll be a lot better than the twerp I have to shut down," I said. "But there's a long back story, and you might as well have a couple of drinks while we talk about it."

"Now, I'm curious. As always. I'll be there," and he hung up.

I texted Mike to make sure my plan was okay with him and thought about what to cook. Couldn't believe I was worrying about tomorrow night's dinner. I decided on make-your-own pizza tonight and chicken tetrazzini tomorrow night. Made a list and headed to the grocery store right after lunch. Keisha assured me, with no little irony, that she was perfectly capable of running the office.

Turns out she wasn't. In fact, she lost it after she came back from lunch and found a note slipped under the door, my name crudely lettered on the envelope. Inside, one of those untraceable notes read, "Your older daughter sure is pretty. Too bad she has to sit alone and wait for you to pick her up after school." Keisha called me immediately, nearly screaming in my ear as I stood in the pasta aisle.

"You got to come see this right now. Leave them blasted groceries. I'll go get them tomorrow."

Alarmed, I asked what was wrong. Were the girls okay?

"Far as I know, but you come quick."

I did that, leaving my basket of groceries and explaining that an emergency called me. A manager assured me he'd restock the groceries, frozen items first. I didn't give a fig about the groceries as I drove too fast to get back to the office and arrived breathless with fear. Keisha was not given to panic.

She made me sit down and then handed me the note, along with latex gloves (we'd learned through bitter experience to keep them on hand). "I've called Mike. He's on his way."

Before I could even read the note, I knew it was like one of my worst dreams come true if she'd called Mike. Keisha acted on that sixth sense, and this time it told her Maggie was in real danger. My eyes didn't linger long over the words. "Call the school. Have them make sure Maggie's in class and have her wait in the office after school."

"Already done," she said, but I noticed she was wringing her hands.

Mike burst in and nearly grabbed the note out of my shaking hands. "I'll go get her."

I shook my head. "Mike, I love you, but she'll be embarrassed if a policeman comes to get her from school. Who knows what her classmates might think?"

"That doesn't matter right now."

I spoke slowly. "I don't think this is a warning for today. It's another harassment to let us know he knows all about our lives. I'll go get her, and Keisha, could you get Em?"

She nodded, and Mike asked, "You have your gun?"

"Yes, but I can't take it into the school."

He rubbed his head. "I could."

"No, we're not going to panic over this, and we're not going to scare the girls. I'll go get her, and I'll be very careful. I'll call when we're all safely home."

He looked doubtful but confiscated the note and stood to leave when I said one more thing.

"We've got to figure out who Charles Sanford and Greg Davis are. I was sure they're one and the same, but now I know they're not. If there are two people, that might be the answer. Sanford is going to represent Jo Ellen North when her father's will goes to probate. Shouldn't he be hiding from me? Isn't there an arrest warrant out for him? But then again, it's not the same Charles Sanford."

Mike shook his head as though to clear it. "Too many players. If Sanford is the one who attacked you, we'll nail him the minute he walks into that courtroom. But you'll have to identify him. What if it's not the same man?"

"How many Charles Sanfords can there be?" I asked.

"The question is how many men can use that name?"

I went to get Maggie. Had to find a parking place, away from the pickup line, so I was a bit late in getting her. She slumped on the bench in the principal's office. At the secretary's request, I signed her out and put an arm around her as we walked out of the office. She shied away.

"Now what's going on," she asked, impatience giving her voice a harsh edge.

"There's sort of been a threat," I said.

"Against me?"

I nodded.

"Okay, Mom. What have you done? I can't wait in the office every day for you. Everyone will laugh at me."

"What if Keisha picks you up?"

"They'd think my nanny was coming for me."

It was the first ever time I'd heard anything like a racial comment, even distinction, from her, and I was suddenly furious. We were all worried about her safety, and she was worried about what other kids would think. I took a deep breath and said, "Let's go for a frozen yogurt."

She didn't say yes or no, so I called Keisha, told her what we were doing, and headed for the yogurt parlor we favored. Once there, I told Maggie carefully, word for word, about the note. Then I said, "All of us are desperately trying to bring this to a conclusion, Maggie. I didn't bring it on us...unless you want to go back to the afternoon Jo Ellen North tried to kill me and you girls saved me."

"But, Mom, it never stops. You always get into some new trouble. You've promised it won't happen, but here we are again."

I played with my napkin. "I know, and I know promising one more time isn't much good. But I think when this baby comes, I'll be a stay-at-home mom and maybe things really will change. In the meantime, we've got to see this one through. And there just might be a bonus in it."

"A bonus?"

I smiled just a bit. "Think of something you really want that's not usually in the budget."

"My own iPad!"

"May just happen. Hang in with me."

Chapter Fifteen

We began a new routine. Keisha still picked Em up, but Maggie waited inside in the office until I came to get her...then she complained bitterly all the way home. Other kids would think she was a runaway, a truant; they were talking about her behind her back. I tried to listen patiently without arguing with her. She never knew that I broke all rules and carried my gun into the school. What if Greg Davis jumped us as we came out? Then again, maybe he'd had enough of my gun.

Keisha had gone to the one-day gun-safety course and passed with a score almost as good as mine, which gave me a twinge of unwelcome jealousy. When I accused her of cheating—tongue-in-cheek—she said, "José been giving me hints." When I suggested she didn't need to carry it to pick up Em, she said righteously, "Now that I have a permit to carry, I'm carrying it all the time. May even get myself one of those fancy purses with a hidden sleeve that makes it easy to get the gun out. There've been times I would have been glad to have it in the office."

I couldn't resist. "You going to carry it at your wedding?"

"Naw. There'll be lots of armed police officers around."

I didn't tell her I doubted they'd be armed.

"That reminds me," she said, "the wedding's in two weeks and two days. We best get serious about planning."

A little late I thought, but it was true—January was moving right along. "Okay, what do we need to do?"

She whipped out a sheet of legal paper. "I got a list." Not at all to my surprise, she had everything covered. Wedding cake—Claire. Minister—her uncle. Music—some boys she went to high school with had a jazz band but assured her they could play the wedding march. They weren't so sure about the traditional recessional, the piece I loved so much. Food—Mona's Bun Appetit cart, Peter to provide sides. Drinks—Peter. Flowers—well, she hadn't thought about that, wanted a bouquet of red roses, with small pink roses for her attendants—that would be Maddie and Em. She didn't much believe in corsages but she thought one would please her mom and then she best get one for José's mom.

"I'llll take care of flowers," I said, making a mental note to request a bouquet for the cake table. We decided against flowers for individual tables.

"What have I forgotten?"

Other than the fact that my daughter was in danger, someone else's daughter was missing, and I was receiving threats, she hadn't left much out. I asked if she knew what her mom and José's mom would wear, and she said, "My mom always wears purple on state occasions. I don't know about his mom."

With a closet full of beige clothes, I decided that would be my color, brightened with a scarf. I didn't have time to order a dress, which I might have done if I'd seen one I fancied. And I had no inclination to go mall shopping. No worry about Mike—he'd wear a suit but I knew he'd have his gun tucked in his belt or in a shoulder holster.

Keisha was silent a long time, staring out the window and apparently collecting her thoughts. "Uh, Kelly, there is one other thing. I sort of hoped you'd bring it up…."

I wracked my brain. What could she be talking about? Finally I looked at her and said, "Help me out."

"That shower you were going to give me. I know we messed things up by hurrying the wedding and all, but ….

"Of course! But in two weeks, when do we have time for a shower?"

"Well, I was hoping you'd change it to a rehearsal…."

"Oh, the night before the wedding?"

"Not exactly. We're taking a week off you know for the honeymoon, so José's got to pick up some extra shifts, and he's working that night. And, of course, he can't see me the day of the wedding…that's bad luck." Now her words were all coming in a rush, and I knew she had everything planned in her mind. "Could we do a rehearsal brunch on Saturday?"

My mind catalogued breakfast casseroles—I'd seen some recipes—and mimosas and Bloody Mary drinks, coffee cake….yes, it was doable, but just barely if I started planning now. Maggie and Em would help me with festive decorations. "Of course we can do that. Just draw up a guest list."

"Just the regulars, plus the minister and my momma and José's parents."

"Where are you staying the night before so José doesn't see you? Your mom's house?"

"Lord no, Kelly. Momma's gonna be so nervous she'd drive me right through the ceiling. I'm staying in your guest house."

Something else to clean and decorate. Suddenly I was tired. The next day was Friday, when I could stay home and make plans and lists and call Claire for help. My mind couldn't quite grasp guns at a wedding, a brunch wedding rehearsal, and Keisha in a wedding dress that I still worried about. This was going to be an amazing event, and I was taking to my bed for a week right afterward.

****

Benjamin Cruze called. The probate hearing was set for the Tuesday before Keisha's wedding. To me, the two events were uncomfortably close, but there was nothing I could do about it. Life was getting more complicated by the moment.

I called Terrell and asked him to put it on his calendar. He suggested we meet beforehand to discuss the case again though we'd been over it the first night he'd come to dinner. Did he just want another meal?

"I have nothing to do with this," Mike said stubbornly. "I didn't know Robert Martin. His bequest is to you, and as long as Terrell is with you, protecting your interests, I'd rather not be there."

"What if Charles Sanford is the man who came after me with a knife?"

"From the lawyer's description, I don't believe he is. I'll have an officer outside the probate court, but believe me, Kelly, the courthouse is crawling with security. All you have to do is holler."

"And what if he's not the same man? How do I know who the real Charles Sanford is?"

"He'll have to present ID to get into the court, so I presume it would be valid…or at least appear to be. Terrell can always request a private moment with the judge."

Terrell had heard all this at our earlier dinner when we explained, as well as we could, the situation, with two men (we thought) named Charles Sanford. However, he wasn't used to the idea of danger in the courtroom and looked increasingly uncomfortable. "I don't have a license to carry," he said.

"No problem," Mike said. "Kelly does."

At that Terrell threw his hands up in the air. "And this Charles Sanford, whoever he is, is representing this Ms. North in court?" he asked incredulously. "Isn't there a warrant out for his arrest?"

"There is," Mike said. "We thought until this court thing came up that he'd gone back to his original identity as Greg Davis and changed his appearance. We haven't been able to find him, although he's obviously been watching us—or someone he's connected to has. Now I don't know what to think but, like you, I doubt he'll show up in court. I think it's someone else named Charles Sanford—or using that name. What we can't any of us figure out is the relationship between Greg Davis, Charles Sanford, and Jo Ellen North."

"You guys sure do make my life interesting," Terrell said.

But what Mike and I both knew from previous experience was that Terrell was very good on his feet and could handle anything that came his way. I wasn't one bit worried about the probate court, beyond that it might be unpleasant, but nagging worries about the wedding continued to bother me. I thought they had to do with Maggie. In my wild, sleepless moments at three in the morning, I imagined her missing on the day of the wedding.

Maggie, meanwhile had adjusted to our new routine and even said one day, "Mom, I'm glad you're always there on cold days, so I don't have to sit and shiver."

I touched her hand. "I'm glad too, Mags." She just didn't know how glad.

****

I went to see the Balcombs the weekend before the wedding, in spite of all that I had to do. I hoped for a clue whether Sandra was held against her will or if she was an active participant in whatever the hell was going on. She could have been the one watching Maggie at the mall or after school. The Balcombs pretty much cancelled that idea for me.

After I was seated and politely declined offers of coffee or tea, Alma could barely get out what she wanted to say. "She called…." and then the mother broke down in tears. After a moment, she wiped her eyes and went on in a quavering voice. "She was whispering, said she didn't know how long she could talk."

"So she found a phone without the knowledge of whoever's with her. Did she say anything important?"

Sticking to facts seemed to give Alma some strength. "She's in a big but dingy old house, and Greg is there along with a woman my age and another man. She's afraid of them, says they're planning something big. She doesn't know what, but she's afraid of what they'll do to her when they pull it off—her words, not mine.'

"Did you ask if she tried to escape?"

"I did, but just then someone shouted, 'You bitch!' and just before the phone went dead I heard the sound of a slap, and Sandra crying aloud. I've been heartsick with worry ever since."

I tried to be patient. "Why didn't you call my husband?"

She studied her knotted hands. "A woman called back right away, but her voice sounded funny…disguised somehow, squeaky and high-pitched and, well, weird."

The same voice disguiser that had been used on the calls to me. "What did she say?" I prompted gently.

"That if I called the police, I'd never see my daughter again. I'm terrified, Miss Kelly. Terrified for Sandra and for all of us."

No need to tell her that I too was terrified for my own daughter.

Joe had sat quietly through this recitation, but now he said, "I told her she should call, that they were just trying to scare her. I can't figure out though if Greg has feelings for our daughter or if somehow she's useful to them. But I think the police should know about the call."

Janice had apparently been listening outside the living room, because she burst into the room, wild-eyed, and almost shouted, "No! You can't tell anyone! You'll ruin everything, and we'll never see Sandra again." Her tone was desperate, pleading, scared.

"Janice, calm yourself," Joe said. "We'll decide what's best in this family."

"But you don't know," she sobbed and ran from the room.

Mike was going to have to find out what Janice was keeping secret.

There was nothing I could do to distract them. I surely didn't want to talk about threats against Maggie, and I doubted they would be interested in the wedding details that occupied my mind. But just for things to say, I prattled on about the upcoming wedding and the brunch planned for the next Saturday.

"That's the kind of thing we'd hoped for Sandra," Alma said sadly, and I wanted to kick myself.

"I'm sure you'll get to plan such things for both your girls. We just have to get through this trial." If I'd been more religious, I might have said God was in charge and holding us in his hands—you see that all the time on Facebook—but I didn't say it. All I could mumble was that Mike would be in touch. As I headed toward the door, I glanced behind me and saw Janice lurking in the dining room.

I headed home in a hurry. Mike was at work on his computer but I didn't even ask if he minded an interruption. I just spit the whole story out in pieces and bits, talking so fast that he held up a hand and said, "Whoa, Kelly. Slow down and start from the beginning."

I tried, told him that my compassionate call had veered into police business, and tried to summarize what seemed important from Sandra's call—the big house, her fear, the voice and the slap. Then I told him about the call Alma got immediately afterward and, finally, about Janice's reaction. "She knows something, Mike. You have to find out what she's so terrified of."

"I'm sure she's terrified for her sister," he said calmly. "But before I go rushing over to the Balcombs, let me try to think this through." Then he winked and said, "I could think better with some lunch. Got any bacon and tomatoes?"

"Sure." I was the little woman being sent to make lunch while the important cop figured things out. *Get over yourself, Kelly!*

The girls clamored to go to Hallmark to buy plates, napkins, and cups for the brunch, all of course with a wedding theme. I promised we'd go after lunch, though I longed for a nap.

A BLT sounded good to me too, and we all enjoyed lunch. The girls were ready to go before I even got the dishes done, but they pitched in and helped. Mike said he was going to the Balcombs' and we'd talk when he got back. Of course, that made me want to rush through the Hallmark trip but that wasn't to be. Do you have any idea how elaborate Hallmark can get—photo albums, guest books, invitations? I explained it was too late for those and Keisha had emailed people. Candles, picture frames, coffee cups, even a Christmas tree ornament with the names of the bride and groom. I had to rein in my daughters big-time, and I vetoed picture frames and Christmas tree ornaments. Even so, it cost a small fortune to get napkins, a guest book, and Styrofoam cups that would be stamped with Keisha and José's name (and I could pick up later—add that to my list).

We went to the liquor store for the clear plastic plates—much more elegant and substantial than the paper wedding-themed ones. While at the liquor store I got champagne for mimosas, Bloody Mary mix, and vodka—not things we ordinarily stocked in our kitchen. I scribbled a note to add orange juice, celery, green onions, to my growing grocery list.

We arrived home laden with bags that made Mike exclaim, "Did you buy out the store?"

"Yes, and there's a case from the liquor store in my car waiting for you to carry it in."

"Mom, you forgot kid wine!" Em was stern.

"I want champagne," Maggie said with dogged determination.

"We'll see, girls. Em, I can get kid wine at the grocery."

Maggie announced that we forgot to get a pretty tablecloth, but I told her our wood table was pretty enough, and I was planning flower arrangements. Little dollar signs were spinning in front of my eyes.

Mike unpacked the liquor store purchases, while the girls stashed all the paper goods on the sideboard in the dining room. "If you girls let me talk to your mom for a minute or so and then let her have a nap, we'll go to Chadra for supper!"

That met with a cheer, so the girls disappeared into their rooms, and Mike and I climbed the staircase to ours. I stretched out on the bed, while he perched on a hassock he'd pulled close to the bed.

"I didn't learn much more from the Balcombs than what you told me, but I do have a trace on their phone. Once again the calls came from the near west side."

"That's a pretty big territory."

"Yeah," he admitted, "but the phone company thinks between Hulen and Montgomery, and the freeway and White Settlement. Doesn't exactly give us a lead but it helps some. I got nothing from Janice Balcomb except what you did. She's terrified, and somehow she feels responsible for her sister's well-being. I told her I could subpoena her, and she almost got hysterical, said if she said anything, her sister is dead. I'm not sure forcing her is the right answer."

I chewed on all this, knowing I'd never be able to quiet my mind enough to nap.

"Kelly, there's just no connection to us and this Greg Davis who has Sandra Balcomb. The only long shot I can think of is Dr. Goodwin's office. Can you call her first thing Monday ask her what she knows about Janice, how Janice has been behaving in the office, and so on. And while you're at it, ask about Mrs. Buxton."

"Why her?" In truth, I wasn't surprised about his tagging Mrs. Buxton, but I wondered how he knew that I had my doubts about her and my high blood pressure readings, along with her recent frequent absences.

He grinned wickedly. "Just my sixth sense. Go to sleep now so you'll be rested for that dinner I promised the girls."

As if I could sleep.

Chapter Sixteen

I called Sherrie Goodwin's office before eight, hoping to get an emergency number and avoid going through Janice. Luck was with me, and I got Sherrie's cell phone. She answered immediately.

"Kelly, what's the matter? Are you all right? It's not like you to call this number."

"I had a reason. Do you have time for a quick cup of coffee at the Old Neighborhood Grill? It's not about my health or my pregnancy. I…I need some information for Mike and a case."

Sherrie was no dummy. "It has to do with Janice's missing sister, doesn't it?"

"Yes…and it's a long shot but you may be able to help us."

"Us?" she echoed.

"Yeah. My family is unfortunately involved."

"Kelly, I've got a full schedule this morning—patients booked from 8:30 to 11:30, but I left a big window for lunch so I could catch up on records. How about if we meet for lunch, and I do my records this evening?"

"I'd be ever so grateful, Dr. Goodwin. If you don't mind, let me serve lunch at my house. I don't want anyone to overhear us."

"Now I'm really curious. I can be there by 12:30 at the latest, maybe a bit earlier. And Kelly, call me Sherrie. None of this doctor stuff, please."

I laughed. Later I'd tell her that had been a dilemma for me. Meantime I gave her the address and said, "See you whenever you can get there."

Mid-morning I told Keisha what was happening and set off to get chicken salad sandwiches and salad from Central Market. Then I whipped home to make sure the house looked decent. I called Mike, told him the plan, and then spent the time waiting for Sherrie by outlining what I wanted to say to her.

When she arrived, I had the table set, plates arranged with sandwiches and salad, along with fresh fruit, and ice water in the glasses. She declined the wine I offered, saying she knew I couldn't drink and she would have to work that afternoon.

She ate and listened; I talked. I began with Janice and the fact that she seemed to know some terrible secret that if she told would put her sister's life in danger. I recounted Sandra's desperate call to her family and Janice's out-of-control reaction to my visit over the weekend.

Sherrie simply commented, "Janice has not been herself ever since the kidnapping. She's edgy, sharp with patients, even difficult with Mrs. Buxton. I've almost mentioned it to her a time or two when she double-booked patients or forgot to register an appointment, but I'm a softie, and I figure she's really hurting."

"I think she is," I said, "but she's not helping us." Then I launched into the story of Greg Davis/Charles Sanford, the inheritance, the threats to my family. "The thing is this Greg Davis seems to know things he shouldn't. Obviously there's a leak somewhere."

"You think there's a mole in my office? Isn't that the term?" She was smiling just a bit, and I smiled back.

"Mike and I think it's a possibility. The other question I have is about Mrs. Buxton. How much do you know about her?"

"I think we talked about this. She came from home health care, was with one elderly man for several years before he died. Said she wanted a change of pace. Recommendations were excellent."

"Do you know the elderly man's name?"

"I suppose I have it in my records but not offhand, no."

"I'm hoping it was Robert Martin, the man who left me the bequest."

She shook her head. "Doesn't sound familiar."

"I hope her attendance record has improved," I ventured.

She shook her head. "No, and I'm going to have to do something about it. I can't operate an office this way, with my nurse practitioner out more than she is in and my receptionist as jumpy as I've ever seen anyone."

I had more questions, and I'd barely touched my sandwich. "Do you know where Mrs. Buxton lives?" I was hoping of course for an address in that wide area the telephone company called west side. I took a bite of my sandwich and waited.

"No. I'd have to look it up, but I can do that, after they're all gone this evening."

My mouth was now full of chicken salad, but I held up one finger. As soon as I could politely talk again, I said, "One more thing. What's the relationship between Janice and Mrs. Buxton?"

She stared off into space. "Funny you should ask. At first, they were good friends, even lunched together, laughed a lot. Now, they're frosty with each other. Mrs. Buxton tries to boss Janice around, and I catch Janice glaring at her, but she never confronts. Since you've told me all this, I've got a lot to think about."

I too had a lot to think about.

****

Sherrie Goodwin called back just after supper. "I'm afraid I don't have much to tell you. I have no record of who Mrs. Buxton cared for. All I have is her references. And her address—she lives on the south side."

My hopes deflated. She wasn't the one making the calls. Nor had she cared for Robert Martin.

"There's one thing that might interest you. One of her references was Charles Sanford, a lawyer. Didn't you mention that name?"

"I did." All kinds of light bulbs went off in my head. "And I'll see Mr. Sanford tomorrow morning in probate court. He's representing Robert Martin's daughter. So, somehow, Mrs. Buxton is tied into the inheritance business. Maybe Mike will know how we find out where she fits into this puzzle of revenge."

So there it was—Janice, Mrs. Buxton, and Greg Davis/Charles Sanford, all tied into the inheritance business and somehow communicating with Jo Ellen North. But how? And who were they? What were their parts?

I grabbed a beer for Mike and headed for the living room, but just as I walked through the archway from the dining area there was an enormous explosion and shattered glass flew into the room. Thinking gunfire, I yelled "Girls, on the floor, flat." They had done this before and obeyed without question, throwing themselves under the table where minutes before they had been peacefully doing homework.

Despite my own warning I stood frozen, staring at a shattered side window, its wooden mullions which once provided a diamond pattern now broken and bent into awkward shapes. Shards and slivers of old-fashioned wavy glass littered the floor. So stunned, I didn't have the sense to get down in case another gunshot came.

Mike meanwhile leapt to his feet, clutching the back of his neck, and went not toward safety but right to the untouched center window—in time to hear a car peel away. I saw blood on the back of his neck, which was enough to unfreeze me and move me toward him.

"Call 911. This will keep."

I did, even while telling Maggie to get a clean cold cloth for Mike. The 911 operator was exasperatingly slow or so it seemed to me. She asked questions and ordered me to stay on the line, over my protests that I needed to tend to my husband.

"How badly is he hurt?"

"His neck is bleeding. I don't know if it's a bullet or flying glass."

Standing near my now, Mike muttered, "No bullet. There's a piece of glass in my neck."

While I tried to remember any major arteries in the back of the neck and couldn't, the operator asked if I heard sirens. I think I would have lied to get off the phone, but I did faintly. She then commanded me to "secure my pets"—secure Gus? He was probably hiding under the bed.

"Maggie, open the front door. Em, go find Gus and lock him in our room." Gus was the most peaceful dog in the world, but I'd heard stories of police shooting first and asking questions later when there was a dog.

Still holding his neck, with a rag against it now, Mike bent down and looked at the floor. "That stupid old rock through a window trick, with a note tied to it."

"What does it say?"

"I'm not picking it up until someone with evidence gloves gets here." He stood when the EMT guys came through the door, carrying their bag. "Glad to see you guys, but no rush. I'll live. Got some glass in my neck when the window broke."

They led him into the kitchen, where they might make less of a mess, and José came through the open door, asking, "What the hell happened here? Who's hurt?"

I explained about Mike and the glass—I seemed to be telling this story a lot—and asked if he could pick up the rock and read the note.

"Sure thing. Be back in a second," and he ran to his patrol car, returned with gloves and the requisite baggie. "Want to place bets?" he asked.

"It's a threat."

He laughed. "Not fair. No way it's a love note." He carefully untied the string and spread the note out on a clean sheet of white paper. The note read:

Last chance to renounce the inheritance. You won't like the consequences by Saturday.

Mike came in, his neck sporting a small bandage, and leaned over José's shoulder. "They won't like the consequences when we catch them." He stared at the note. "It's disguised handwriting but obviously feminine. A new player."

"Not so new," I said. "It's either Sandra or Mrs. Buxton. Sherri Goodwin just called. She didn't find much in her files that was helpful except that a lawyer named Charles Sanford was one of Mrs. Buxton's references. I'd swear that the Charles Sanford I met was neither old enough nor smart enough to be a lawyer. There are two people using that name."

"I think you're right, but you'll find out tomorrow."

"What do I do if he isn't the same person? In fact, what do I do if it is the same person?"

"Nothing except keep your cool. Benjamin Cruze will defend the will as written, and Terrell will represent you. Nobody will take a knife after you in the courthouse."

Small comfort, I thought.

****

Terrell came for coffee the next morning, claiming he'd already had breakfast but wanted to escort me to the courthouse. Since I was a basket of nerves, I was grateful. If he noticed that my hand shook when I poured his coffee, he said nothing. I had eaten a few small bites of oatmeal, but my stomach was churning. I never liked going to court, the few times I'd had to do it, but the thought of Charles Sanford made me all the more nervous.

We sat on a wooden bench outside the probate court until we were called. Terrell, Benjamin Cruze, and I were on one bench. I introduced Terrell, and Cruze said polite things to both of us. Then he turned to me and in *sotto voce* said, "You don't have anything to worry about."

This was still a dilemma for me: was I right to accept money from a man I barely knew, if at all, and whose life I had ruined, no matter what he said in his will?

A middle-aged man, slightly rumpled, graying hair, arrived and spoke to Benjamin. They shook hands, and Benjamin introduced Terrell and me to Charles Sanford. I stood and gaped, barely able to offer a hand

and mutter, "Nice to meet you." This Charles Sanford was someone I'd never met. He was pretty much as Benjamin Cruze described him.

I couldn't believe this was the man who wanted me dead. Not just withdrawn from the inheritance, but dead. I recovered myself enough to look into his eyes, but I didn't see the steely-eyed killer I expected. They were pale blue, watery, neutral—not particularly kind but certainly not menacing. He moved on to Terrell whom he seemed to know, and they shook hands cordially as acquaintances will do.

We each sat down on our respective benches again, and Sanford began pulling papers out of a scuffed brief case and studying them. I watched him, but he never looked at me, and if he knew who I was, he gave no indication. Yet, something about him made me think he lacked cunning…and I had known some cunning people. I couldn't quite figure him out.

I wanted to ask Benjamin questions, but we were too close to the others. I wanted to know if he was with a firm or in private practice. Certainly, he wasn't Robert Martin's lawyer—Benjamin represented that firm. So how did he come to represent Jo Ellen, who was supposedly not contacting anyone? And why had he let Greg Davis use his name? Or maybe Greg Davis used it without his knowledge. I sat and stewed.

Neither Benjamin nor Terrell seemed to need to review papers, so they chatted about legal matters, their talk going around me and over my head.

Finally we were called into the small courtroom. Judge MacDonald was a portly older man with outright white hair and eyes that shone with kindness. There was no grief in this courtroom today, but I suspected over years of dealing with probate he had seen too much grief and too much greed and developed empathy for people. Today there was only greed, a thought that made me cringe.

After introduction, the judge said, "I understand, Mr. Cruze, you have the latest will, countersigned by you in the presence of an independent notary and witnesses."

"Yes, your honor."

"And you were present when Mr. Martin dictated the codicil?"

"Yes, sir."

"How was his mental state?"

"He was physically frail, but mentally alert. He seemed quite determined that Ms. O'Connell had helped him and that his daughter had caused him great humiliation—that was his word."

"Did you try to dissuade him?"

"No, sir that was not my duty. One of the witnesses did speak to him confidentially until I reminded her she was there as an independent witness, not to influence the proccedings. I'm pretty sure she was speaking on behalf of Mr. Martin's daughter and against the proposed change of the will. She was his nurse, a woman named Buxton. Mr. Martin told her his daughter would still get half of his estate, which is sizeable—in fact he said it was more money than she'd ever need if she survives her prison term. It will be held in a trust for her for the rest of her lifetime, after which he has designated several charities."

My mind was still reeling with the knowledge that Mrs. Buxton had been, as we suspected, Robert Martin's nurse.

The judge nodded. "Yes, I'm familiar with the background of this case." He turned toward me. "Ms. O'Connell, did you wish to address the court?"

Terrell and I had talked about this and decided I should not speak. I could have rambled on forever about blood money, guilt money, and my error in taking it. On the other hand, I could have explained that I believed Mr. Martin was giving it as a legacy to my daughters in the hope that they would turn out differently than his daughter. All I said was, "No, thank you," which earned me a sharp, sudden look from Mr. Sanford.

Just then, the judge turned toward him. "Mr. Sanford, I don't believe I've seen you in my court before."

"No, sir, your honor. I'm a tax lawyer and don't generally do probate work. I'm doing this as a favor to a friend."

"Pro bono? Not that it matters."

"Yes, sir, as a matter of fact. My friend is not in a position to pay legal fees at the time."

"And your friend or client is Jo Ellen North, who is contesting the will. Am I right?"

"Yes, sir. Mrs. North believes with her...er...unavailable, her father was coerced into adding this codicil."

There it was. Right out in the open.

"By whom?"

"She is not sure. She thinks perhaps it was his nurse." Turning to Benjamin, he asked, "Was that the woman who spoke to him?"

Benjamin had his mouth open to say, "Yes," when the judge said, "Mr.Sanford, please address the court. Mr. Cruze, regard the question as irrelevant." Turning back to Sanford, "Is your client angry at Ms. O'Connell? Remember I know the background here. I believe your client killed Ms. O'Connell's ex-husband, tried to kill her, and threatened her children."

"Yessir, all that is true. And, yes, Mrs. North is very bitter about Ms. O'Connell because she hashed up a scandal that had been hidden for many decades."

"Angry enough to object to the codicil?"

I wanted to shout, *Angry enough that she wants to kill me or my daughter!* Terrell's restraining hand was on my arm.

"She feels after she cared for her father and hid her mother's secret all these years, it's only just that she inherit the entire estate."

"She does realize that she won't be eligible for parole until she's an old woman, if then?"

"Yes, she does. And she knows she gets only a small allowance monthly as long as she's in prison."

"All right then, back to coercion. What proof does she have?"

Again, I wanted to jump into the fray and shout, *Only her demented state of mind,* but Terrell restrained me.

"She believes that since the codicil was signed well over a year after she was imprisoned and therefore had no contact with her father, he was vulnerable to persuasion. He was unable to travel to Gatesville to see her so she had no influence on him. Sort of out of sight, out of mind."

My inner voice said, *And oh my, did she influence him when she was around him.* Terrell didn't even have to hold me back that time.

After lengthy discussion, during which it was clear Mr. Sanford didn't have a lot of supporting evidence, the judge retired to his quarters, asking us to wait.

"Usually," Benjamin whispered, "he takes a day or two. This is a good sign."

Within an hour, the judge was back and announced that the codicil would stand. He signed some papers, a notary made them official, and the lawyers packed up to leave. Although we seemed to have been there for hours, it was only 11:30.

Mr. Sanford slunk away, without speaking, looking defeated and worried. Maybe he was afraid of Mrs. Buxton or Greg Davis or both.

I sat stunned, as though I was hearing again a crashing noise—a rock through a window, a threat now come to reality.

"Kelly?" Terrell asked gently. "You coming with us?"

I pulled myself together and smiled up at him. "Of course." If he noticed my paleness, my troubled expression, he was good enough not to mention it.

The three of us left together, Terrell carefully taking my elbow to be sure I didn't fall down the entire length of the steep courthouse stairs.

"Lunch?" Terrell suggested. We all agreed and headed for a restaurant on the new Sundance Square. Since it was a cold, January day, we opted for an upstairs table where we could look out over the square.

We were barely seated when I pounced on Benjamin, but before I even got my question out, he said, "The woman who talked to Robert Martin was his nurse." His eyes glinted with laughter because he'd known that question was on my mind since he'd mentioned the incident. "But why would she be so interested in having you inherit?"

"I don't think she is. If anything, she'd be interested in Jo Ellen getting all the money, hoping then that Jo Ellen would remember her kind care of her father."

"Did Mrs. Buxton work there before all the trouble started? Would she have known Jo Ellen?"

I shrugged. "I suspect so because from what I understand from Mrs. Buxton's current employer is that she took care of an elderly man for several years."

I sank back into myself. More parts of the puzzle were falling into place—principally Mrs. Buxton. *But how and where did Charles*

Sanford fit in? And why had Greg Davis used his name the day he tried to kill me? In fact, how did Greg Davis and the Balcomb sisters fit in, because now I was convinced they both did?

"Terrell, you seemed to know Charles Sanford. What do you know about him?"

He shrugged. "Just a two-bit courthouse lawyer. Sometimes hangs around hoping to get a case. Office is downtown in one of those old buildings across from the courthouse. He's not...uh...a power. I've just met him a couple of times. Never been in court with him before."

Benjamin spoke up. "He doesn't seem to be much of a presence. Don't worry, Kelly. It's over and done. Half the estate goes to you. What will you do? I imagine after taxes you have just under two million. Robert Martin was worth a lot more than that in years past, but time and the government haven't been kind to him."

Two million dollars! I thought about it. Slowly, I said, "I'd like to give some to Marie Winton's family—she's the young woman Martin's wife shot and killed. Her family knew nothing of what happened to her for forty years or more, and I think helping them is a fitting tribute to her. Beyond that, I'd give some to the Edna Gladney Home, which could have helped Marie Winton and did help Lorna MacDavid, and I'd boost the college fund for the girls and the new baby...and who knows what else."

The thought of the new baby made me cringe. It was almost time for another checkup, and I did not want to see Mrs. Buxton. Ever again if I could help it! I shuddered thinking about it.

"Kelly," Terrell said. "Come back. Where did you go? We're ready to order lunch."

"Sorry. I was off in space for a minute. Must have been

Benjamin's question about all that money." They both ordered cheeseburgers, and I picked at a salad. When Terrell ordered a beer, I truly debated a glass of wine—one glass, when I was almost in the third trimester—surely it wouldn't hurt. I settled for iced tea.

What lingered in the back of my mind—more than the baby, and more than the questions about Greg Davis and Mrs. Buxton and Charles Sanford—was that crashing rock, the threat that hung over our heads now that my acceptance of the inheritance was finally a reality. When would the next shoe drop? And how many shoes were there? I didn't mention it to my companions, not even to Terrell on the way home.

What I needed to think about more was the shower and wedding this weekend...uh, four days away.

Chapter Seventeen

As Keisha had threatened, the invitation had gone out two weeks before the event, and I began to think email was a good idea. Greg or whoever couldn't pilfer out of a mailbox to find out the date and place. Of course if he was also an accomplished hacker....*Don't go, there, Kelly. The gods can only stack the cards against you so much.*

Keisha had called lazy responders and bullied them into answering, until we had a guest list of nearly forty. Claire was baking hearty breakfast casseroles with sausage, cheese, bread, eggs, cream of mushroom soup—everything but the kitchen sink. We figured we needed four. My mom surprised me by offering to make cinnamon coffee cakes—for a moment I was carried back in time to when she made them for me as a child. I hadn't seen her make one in years, but she said making four would be no problem. I was amazed and grateful.

Anthony offered to bring fruit, if Theresa would arrange the platter, and Joe, admitting to stints as a bartender, would take care of making Bloody Marys, mimosas, and pouring soft drinks, kid wine, and other non-alcoholic beverages. We'd have white wine for the few who wanted it.

Sheila O'Gara surprised me by calling and offering to do the flowers. "I never told you," she said, "but that was one of my hobbies. I took some classes and got pretty good at it. I'd be pleased to do that for

Keisha—she was so good to me." We hadn't seen Sheila and her partner, Don, much since the birth of Sheila's baby, and I just guessed they were all wrapped up in caring for an infant and exploring their own new relationship. As I accepted her kind offer, it occurred to me that this was the first big event, the first "gala" that Ms. Lorna, her mother, would miss. My breath suddenly left me.

"Kelly? Are you there? Can I come walk through the house and see where you'll need flowers?"

I breathed deeply, wondering if she felt what I did. "Of course." We arranged she would come on Thursday night and do the flowers Friday so they'd be fresh Saturday morning.

After school Wednesday, the girls and I went to The Party Warehouse, where you could get the most amazing party supplies for not the family fortune—we chose bright turquoise plastic flatware, good plastic wine glasses whose stems did not separate from the glass at unfortunate times, smaller glasses for non-alcoholic drinks, balloons, streamers, banners that proclaimed Happy Wedding. We should have forgotten Hallmark and come here first. All that schmaltz didn't really appeal to me, but I knew Keisha would love it.

Our guests would mostly have to eat standing up but it couldn't be helped, and only the bravest would venture outside. Claire and I rearranged furniture a thousand times, trying to maximize space. Claire brought Liz and Brandon with her to move furniture—I was only allowed to direct. My "delicate condition" had some advantages, I reasoned. Finally we had it the way we thought would allow the best traffic flow. We had just settled down with wine for Claire, Perrier for me and Liz (who protested she'd prefer a beer), when Mike came in and demanded, "What the hell happened to my house?"

"Our house," I said gently. "We're getting ready to have Coxey's Army for breakfast Saturday, remember?"

Keisha had been responsible for inviting family, including the minister, her mother, her sisters and some aunts, uncles, cousins I'd never heard of and who apparently weren't coming to the wedding.

"Are you close to all of them?" I asked weakly.

"No, honey, not hardly any of them. But you know how folks is—leave one out and it grows from there to a whole big snowball." I upped Claire to five casseroles, Mom to five coffee cakes ("Oh, dear, Kelly!") and called the Party Warehouse for more supplies to be delivered Friday. Then I collapsed in bed, utterly exhausted at 5:30, and slept the clock around.

By Friday night I was fairly confident. Everything seemed in order, so much so that Mike made supper—a favorite chicken casserole—and told me to stay off my feet. I had to admit my ankles were swollen, my low back ached, and it felt terrific to sit on the couch with my feet on the coffee table.

"Mom," Maggie remonstrated, "you don't let us put our feet on the coffee table."

"You're not almost six months pregnant," I replied serenely.

As we ate our dinner in the living room, another daily "no-no," Em asked, "Is Keisha coming over to preview everything?" The room was strewn with streamers and banners, and bouquets of balloons hung from various places. A lovely flower arrangement decorated the dining table, and smaller arrangements were scattered around on coffee tables and bookcases. It really did look festive.

"No, she wants to be surprised," I said.

I turned in early, knowing I'd have to be up early, and as I drifted off I heard Mike and Maggie in a heated chess game. Em was no doubt entertaining herself with a design problem. And I was completely content with my world. There had been no threat, and now I thought Greg Davis or whoever was all bluster and hot air. Maggie was safe. I slept soundly.

Next morning, we were having an early breakfast when José burst in through the kitchen door. "Where's Keisha?" he demanded. "I figured she came over here to spend the night but she's not out in the garage apartment."

Mike held up a hand. "She's not at your apartment?"

"Nope. But as I said I just figured she was over here, so I went to sleep, got up early and came to surprise her. But she's not out there…and she's not in here." He looked around the kitchen as though to confirm this conclusion.

"Slow down, man. We haven't seen her since yesterday. She didn't want to come over here last night because she wants to be surprised." Mike paused a minute. "Where's her car?"

"Right where she always parks it."

"Purse?"

"On the coffee table. She always throws it there when she comes in. Her high-heeled shoes are by it too."

"You call her mom?"

He shook his head. "I don't want to scare her. Keisha doesn't run home to mama unless it's something big…like deciding she doesn't want to marry me."

"She's not going to do that, José. She's crazy about you." I volunteered.

"Something bad has happened. I know it."

Mike stood leaning against the counter, his thought processes almost showing on his face. "Let's think this through. She should be here…in fact, she should be at this house in about an hour. She's not home. Did you check the office?"

"No. I kind of panicked because I was so sure she'd be here…and then she isn't. I'll go check that now." He started to rise.

"Sit down," Mike commanded. "I'll have someone go by there. Kelly, you call Keisha's mom. Say she told you she was going to run some errands and you need to ask her something. Did she by any chance run by there? We don't want to alarm her."

Keisha's mom was a blank. She hadn't seen or heard from her but didn't seem the least concerned. "My girl, she's got a mind of her own. I'll see you all shortly."

The neighborhood officer on duty declared the office was locked and dark and empty.

The girls were sitting speechless, listening to all this. Finally Em wailed, "Is Keisha all right? I'll die if anything happens to her." She swept a dramatic arm across her forehead.

Maggie looked at her. "How do you think José feels?"

The question was designed to put Em in her place but was ineffective.

"Awful," Em said as she ran around the table to give him a huge hug.

"José," Mike interrupted. "Any sign of a struggle? Anything out of the ordinary you noticed?"

He shook his head. "I wasn't thinking like a cop, Mike. I was just looking for my lady."

"Okay, that's the first place we stop." Over his shoulder, he shouted, "Kelly, call Peter. Make sure she's not stuffing herself at the Grill."

I'll strangle her if she is, with all the food we're about to have in this house! Peter hadn't seen her all morning.

"But I'll see you all in a bit," he said. "I don't think I've ever been to a shower before. You know, men aren't usually invited."

I assured him we'd be glad to see him and hung up more abruptly than I meant. By now, I was scared. Deep down in the bones kind of scared. The girls clung to me, though Maggie made a show of comforting me, while Em more openly needed comfort for herself. I wandered around the kitchen, unable to think of what I should do next. The girls, well trained by now, rolled flatware into the napkins and set it all in a basket next to a pile of plates. Then they filled pitchers with ice water, put plastic plates under them to avoid dripping condensation, and put the pitchers on the table. Maggie even sliced a lemon into each pitcher. All I managed to do was turn the oven onto warm.

Claire arrived followed by Liz and Brandon who each carried a casserole. Claire took one look at me and asked, "Omigosh, what's wrong?"

"Keisha's missing," I said.

She almost dropped the casserole she was carrying. "Kelly, if this is some kind of a wedding joke...."

"It's no joke," I said miserably. "I wish it were."

I told her the full story, as much as I knew, and said Mike and José had gone back to the apartment to "study" things. "What should we do?" I asked, literally wringing my hands.

"You should sit down right here." Having set her casserole down, she pulled out a kitchen chair and then another one for my feet.

"We will proceed as if nothing is wrong. Kids, put those casseroles in the oven and then go back for the other two. They won't all fit, but we'll figure out something. Maggie, Em, you've done a great job with decorations and tables. Looks perfect."

Claire completely took charge, handling all the food as various people arrived. Everyone seemed to take the news of missing Keisha quite calmly, and Anthony summed it up when he said, "She'll be back in time for the rehearsal."

Mike called. The report was not helpful. "No sign of a struggle, her purse is still here. I'm pretty sure she's been kidnapped, but why Keisha? Why not you, since you get the inheritance? Or why not Maggie, as they kept threatening, because she's the way to your heart?"

I drew another of those deep breaths. "Because you've been here, protecting Maggie and me. And because they know I care deeply about Keisha."

We hung up, and I sat and thought. No one would have taken Keisha against her will without a terrific struggle. I knew that much about her. I knew she was a fighter. Hadn't she always bragged she could handle anyone who came after us? What about a gun? I suspect Keisha would have called their bluff, said, "Go ahead and shoot," and lunged for the gun, disarming them. So how did someone kidnap Keisha?

I picked up my cell phone to call Mike and noticed a text message. It was from Keisha and read simply, "Nusre" and then nothing.

"Nusre?" from my super-skilled typist office manager. What was wrong with her that she couldn't spell "Nurse" and why would she be sending me that message? It didn't take a nanosecond: Nurse meant Mrs. Buxton. She had something to do with Keisha's disappearance.

I called Mike, my fingers almost as clumsy as Keisha's had been

because I was frantic. I didn't even give him time to say, "Shandy."
Instead I rushed on, "Mike, look for glasses…probably wine, maybe beer
bottles, anything that indicates two people had a drink. If there are
more….I don't think I want to know about it." Keisha wouldn't
knowingly drink with the enemy, yet she knew enough to be suspicious
of Mrs. Buxton. But I bet Keisha, being Keisha, thought she could outwit
her. Maybe this time she outwitted herself.

"Kelly, we're outside, looking for signs of a scuffle or fight
around her car. We think maybe she was jumped before she ever got into
the apartment."

"Then why were her shoes in the apartment?"

Long silence. I didn't say "I told you so"—honest I didn't, but I
told him about the message and my theory.

"We're on it. Call you right back."

It was maybe four minutes when he called to say, "Two wine
glasses, traces of red wine. We bagged it all. Lab will analyze wine for
sedative, check glasses for prints."

"All that will take too long. Mike, we need Keisha here in an
hour."

He had his patient tone on. "Kelly, Keisha's safety is more
important than her shower."

I didn't say, "Not to Keisha," but I thought it. "This is her dream
weekend. We can't let it be ruined."

"I don't know what we can do except follow police procedures.
We'll send someone to the address Sherrie Goodwin gave us for Mrs.
Buxton, and someone to the Balcombs. I think maybe they need
protection anyway."

Long shots, I thought, and not what's needed right now.

Meantime, everyone who brought food was congregating in the kitchen, and more guests were straggling in. I greeted Keisha's mom and the uncle, or was it great-uncle, who would perform the ceremony, hastily explaining that Keisha would be a bit delayed, but I was going to get her now. Then I drew Claire aside and whispered what was going on. "Please make guests welcome and comfortable…and give them lots to drink so they don't get antsy." Of course, Keisha's mom didn't drink and might worry herself into a tizzy if I didn't hurry.

"Where are you going?"

"To get Keisha."

"Without Mike? Kelly, you can't…."

"Mike is duty bound to arrive with squad cars, flashing lights, all that. I can do this myself and no one will get hurt."

She looked more than doubtful, but I turned and ran upstairs to get my gun, kissed the girls and told them I'd be right back and meantime help Claire, and ran out the door—only to run smack into Terrell Johnson.

"Just the person I need," I said, grabbing his hand. "Come with me." And I ran for my car.

Thinking it was all a joke, he laughed and said, "What? We're going to drag the reluctant bridegroom here?"

"No. We're going to rescue the kidnapped bride."

He sobered and snapped himself into the passenger seat without another word.

I peeled out of the driveway at a speed that made Terrell clutch his armrest. It wasn't until I was on Eighth Avenue, headed for the freeway, that he managed to ask, "Where is she? And how do you know?"

"In a house in River Crest, and I know by instinct."

"Did you call Mike?"

Once again, I explained. "Mike would come with multiple cars, sirens blaring, lights blazing. There'd be a standoff. Someone might get shot. I have to get Keisha back to my house in an hour." I said a silent prayer that she wasn't still doped up.

Terrell was visibly alarmed. "I always said you made my life interesting. I'm not sure I want it this interesting. How are we going to do this?" He wiped his forehead with a nervous hand.

"I'll know when I get there."

All I got in reply was a huge sigh.

I sped to the Ashland exit and wove through the Arlington Heights neighborhood until I reached Camp Bowie, where I had to double back a bit to get to River Crest Drive. Then I slowed to a sedate speed and cruised by the house at 1305 River Crest. Two cars stood in the driveway, neither of them familiar—one a small, oldish Honda and the other a Jeep. I drove around the block.

"Terrell, I'm going to let you out. The curtains are all drawn, so I think you can sneak down the driveway…"

"Now, let's think this through, Kelly…."

"I have. You can let the air out of two tires of each vehicle. Stay low." I pulled just past the driveway, and Terrell eased out of the car. As he gently closed the door, I said, "Keep your gun handy." He gave me a dirty look.

I drove down the block, parked, and walked back, trying for all the world to look like I was out for a casual Saturday stroll. At the driveway to the late Robert Martin's house, I eased along the edge of the bushes between the drive and the next property, then quickly crossed to the back door. It had a glass pane, curtained, but it was unlocked. The door opened into an old-fashioned back porch—a stoop, Keisha would have said—with barely enough room for an ancient refrigerator. On my left was the door into the kitchen, also glass-paned but covered with a sheer curtain that gave me some advantage. I stayed motionless, trying to figure out who was where. Greg Davis and Mrs. Buxton sat at opposite ends of the table, both turned away from me toward the person in the middle. The young blond girl could be no one else but Sandra Balcomb. She was good—a flick of the eyes told me she saw me but other than that she stifled any reaction.

I pulled out my gun, grateful for once to have the loathsome thing. With what I hoped was one sudden, swift motion, I threw open the door and yelled, "Nobody move!" Greg Davis, of course, moved, jumping up to confront me. Sandra Balcomb did an amazing thing—she reached down, grabbed his leg with both hands and pulled back as hard as she could. Davis went splat, face down, directly in front of me. For good measure, I reached down and hit him fairly hard with the gun butt. He was out.

Mrs. Buxton, meantime, had run through a door into the house. Within seconds, I heard a scream that was shortly cut off, and Keisha emerged, pushing Mrs. Buxton in front of her and holding tight to a rope around the older woman's neck. Mrs. Buxton clawed at the rope and tried futilely to kick behind her but Keisha was too much and too quick for her.

Keisha eyed me and asked, "What took you so long? I was gettin' real tired of this place and these people."

I didn't know whether to laugh or cry.

Just then Terrell burst through the door, tripped over the still-unconscious Davis, righted himself, and asked, "Did I miss all the fun?"

Sandra Balcomb wailed, "I want to go home," while Keisha plopped Mrs. Buxton into a chair and carefully tied her hands behind the back of the chair.

"Just finished untying myself with this," she said philosophically. "Might as well put it to good use."

Sandra said her first helpful thing. "I know where there's more."

"Get it," Keisha commanded, having taken charge of the situation. Keisha would always be Keisha.

Sandra returned with rope and got a butcher knife for cutting it. Terrell hauled a groggy Davis into the chair he'd been sitting in and tied his arms behind him. Then he tied his feet to the chair and did the same to Mrs. Buxton, who was now protesting loudly.

"You can't do this! Jo Ellen will be furious."

"Jo Ellen? She has no power. You might remember that," I said.

"But she'll have money," the woman cried.

Davis gave her a dirty look.

And I knew that what I suspected was right all along.

I went back into command mode. "Sandra, we'll get you home as soon as we can. Terrell is a good guy, and he'll keep you safe." Turning to him, I said, "You stay here with these lovely folks. Give us a ten-minute head start and then call Mike. Tell him I'm taking Keisha to her bridal shower."

Keisha practically pulled me out the door. "What're we waiting for?" Then she complained because I'd parked so far away.

I ignored her, rushing as fast as I could to keep up as she nearly ran down the block. Nope, she wasn't drugged.

Chapter Eighteen

Keisha, in yesterday's tired muumuu and flat shoes, was the belle of the ball. We were only a little late for the party, so most guests didn't know, and few would question Keisha's sartorial choices. I whispered, "I'll explain later" to the girls and Claire.

Mike called, and I had to take the phone upstairs to avoid sharing his anger with the whole crowd. He called me harebrained, foolish, headstrong, and accused me of endangering our unborn baby. I listened meekly, and when he finally calmed down, he said, "Good job, Kelly. But absolutely against the law—breaking and entering among other charges. And in spite of what you told Terrell, I would have had the sense to come without screaming sirens and flashing lights."

After a pause—I think he had to catch his breath—he asked, "How did you know where she was?"

I explained that one time Sandra Balcomb had been able to call her parents, and she'd said something about a big, old-fashioned house and an older woman being there. "It just clicked this morning. And I honestly would have called you, but you'd have held Keisha for questioning, and she'd have missed her own party."

He sighed. "You're probably right. I'd have had to. I can hold these folks on charges of kidnapping Sandra Balcomb, but I'll have to question Keisha before they leave for a honeymoon."

"I can't think that far ahead. I have to get back downstairs for the shower."

"Kiss the bride for me and tell her I'm sending her groom there now. He's useless around here. I probably won't get there."

José and Terrell arrived together, joking that they were on parole but not dismissed. Keisha threw her arms dramatically around José who said how worried he'd been about her. She drew back,

"Honey, I can take care of myself. You know that. Why I singlehandedly subdued that wicked Buxton woman."

I kept very quiet.

After that, José was almost the forgotten man as the guests ate heartily, and Claire's casseroles all but disappeared. Joe kept busy dispensing lots of Bloody Marys and mimosas, plus white wine. Otto was the first to toast the bride and groom, an Old World toast that I thought was sweet but made Maggie giggle. Sort of a German version of the Irish, "May the road rise to meet you."

José's father was still puzzled that his son was called José and not Joe, as he was known at home. But he gallantly rose to toast Keisha, the most welcome new member of his family. Keisha rushed to hug her father-in-law. After that toasts came one after another—from Terrell, from Anthony who turned his into a slight poke at Keisha's bossiness, and even from me—standing in for Mike.

Keisha had a mountain of gifts to open—she had registered every place from Target to Neiman Marcus, and I was relieved at least that she hadn't registered at Babies R Us—though I guessed I soon should. She oohed and aahed over everything, a toaster/oven, a Keurig coffeemaker, sheets and towels, the stainless steel flatware she had chosen, and several settings of her everyday china. Predictably she eschewed fine china, saying, "I ain't never gonna serve on that stuff. But I need a whole lot of the everyday stuff."

The girls, having been trained by their mother, scurried around picking up wrappings and ribbons that Keisha flung in every direction and Theresa showed them how to fashion the ribbons through a paper plate to make a faux bouquet. She also quietly kept count of the number of ribbons Keisha broke. When the flurry of present opening was over, Theresa announced that in her haste to get to the contents, Keisha had broken eleven ribbons—she and José would have eleven children.

Keisha arched an eyebrow at her fiancé, and he blushed to the roots of his hair.

Then came the wedding rehearsal. None of the guests wanted to leave, so everyone stood around. Keisha' s nephew walked her down the aisle—an adorable boy of about sixteen who took his responsibility seriously—and José waited by her uncle, the rather elderly minister who would perform the ceremony. The minister was…ah…inventive. He'd quote a bit of the Bible and then go off on a tangent of his own on marital fidelity or the glories of parenthood or the importance of solving all disagreements before going to bed. In short, he rambled. Unmercifully. When he finally asked, "Who giveth this woman," Keisha stepped boldly forward and said, "I do. I give myself to this man." Even her uncle looked startled.

For the rehearsal we had no way to work music in, but even so it lasted an hour. The next day's ceremony would be endless, and frankly, I was already exhausted. Gradually the guests began to drift away with cries of, "See you tomorrow."

Bless Claire. She saw that I'd pushed myself too hard. "You sit right there. We'll get this cleaned up in a flash."

It wasn't a flash. It was more like two hours, with Brandon, Liz and Megan helping, Mom fluttering in the kitchen, Otto dozing in his favorite chair, and Terrell doing whatever he could to be helpful. Keisha and José were told they could not help, but they did. When all was done, there was a mountain of trash and few leftovers—always the sign of a successful party.

Mike came home just as the cleanup wound down, and Keisha gave him a plate of leftovers that he ate ravenously. But we all hung on his words, and soon we were clamoring to hear the story.

"Keisha should tell the first part," he said. "What do you remember about Friday night?"

Keisha herself was beginning to show the strain of what she'd been through. The high that carried her through the day was wearing off, and she sank down on the couch next to me. "I hadn't been home long...maybe an hour...when the doorbell to our apartment rang. I don't know who I expected, but it wasn't Mrs. Buxton. There she was, with a story about being so worried about the Balcomb girls. Did I know anything more? I said no, but my mama raised me right...."

I was glad her mama had left with the crowd and wasn't hearing this story.

"So I invited her in. She really seemed upset, and I felt sorry for her. She said a little wine would calm her nerves. Did I have any and would I join her. So I was puzzled but couldn't see any trouble in that, so I got out a bottle of red and served us both. Then I went back to the kitchen to find some cheese and crackers, and we sat and talked about Sandra and what could that awful boy have done with her, and she said Janice was so upset she was cross in the office these days.

"After that things go a little fuzzy. I remember feeling really hot and fanning myself…and I couldn't really understand what she was saying. My own answers didn't seem to come out sensible, but she kept talking. First thing I know she takes the glasses to the kitchen and fills them again. I told her I really didn't think I needed anymore, but she said it would make me feel better. I think what she said was, 'You look a little pale.' Hah! If I'd had my wits about me, I'd have known I never look pale.

"I guess I passed out but I do remember her and someone else kind of half carrying me, half walking me down the steps and helping me into a car. I woke up…must have been the middle of the night, maybe even on towards morning, tied to a chair in someone's old-fashioned dining room with a lace tablecloth on a big, long table and heavy drapes at the window. My head hurt like it's never hurt before. I don't think I'll ever drink wine again."

"Did they talk to you once you were awake?" Mike asked.

"Nope. I pretended to still be asleep. Scared 'em. They talked maybe they'd given me too much and killed me, but that old Buxton woman swore she knew what she was doing. Then they sent that Sandra in to give me sips of coffee—awful coffee! And she fed me one of those breakfast bar things, tasted like cardboard.

"Can you tell me anything else?"

"Sure I can, Mike. I got real good ears. They were in the kitchen, but they were yelling at each other—some about what to do with me, now they got me. That Davis boy kept telling Buxton she wasn't going to get her hands on that money, and she said she just needed time to think. She kept calling someone—Jo Ellen, I'm sure—who told her to off me. She had no qualms but Greg Davis kept saying he didn't sign on for murder. Sandra kept quiet as a mouse. I think she's like those abused women you hear about—she could have escaped but Davis bullied her until she was too scared to do anything. So she just tried to stay invisible. Maybe she was afraid they'd kill her too."

"She's been reunited with her family," Mike said. "More tears than I've seen in a while. That's one problem child who may now be on the right path, but she'll need lots of counseling. We'll talk to her again next week, but for now I thought it best for her to be with her family. Keisha, I'm afraid you'll have to postpone your honeymoon until we get this all cleared up."

Keisha sighed. "I ain't surprised."

Mike told us that Mrs. Buxton was the brains behind this whole scheme. She was Mr. Martin's nurse for years, so Jo Ellen knew her. "Davis is just a petty criminal who happens to be her nephew. And Charles Sanford is her brother—she bullied him into doing her so-called legal work. Quite a family.

"Anyway, Jo Ellen set the whole thing in motion, promising them a huge reward if they could get you to turn down your share of the inheritance. She must have had a disposable cell phone she used to call Mrs. Buxton. The thing she didn't tell them was that she won't have access to the money—she couldn't give them any if she wanted to. And they weren't smart enough to figure that out. "

"Such greed," Claire said.

"I don't think it's greed, Claire. I think she has an unreasonable hate for me. I don't know that I'll ever feel completely safe from her scheming," I said. "Keisha, I'm so sorry this happened to you, but I'm so glad they didn't touch Maggie."

"Can I go to the mall with friends now?" Maggie asked.

I didn't think she realized the enormity of what she escaped.

Maybe there was no sense in scaring her to death. "Negotiable," I said.

"The reason they got Keisha instead is because we kept such a close watch on Maggie. They knew Keisha would matter to you too," Mike said. "But they sure underestimated you."

"In a way, they didn't, Mike," Keisha said. "That Buxton thing talked about how Jo Ellen wanted them to kill you too, Kelly…."

I shivered.

"And once she said you don't scare easy. She'd tried with that blood pressure business, trying to scare you with the possibility of eclampsia but you didn't panic. She was real disappointed in that."

"Keisha, you sure heard an earful while you were drugged," I said with a nervous laugh.

"Trouble is," Keisha said, "I think I gave her too much information while we were having our drinks and I was beginning to feel…uh, loose. I know I told her all about the wedding, where and when it would be, how excited I was."

Mike still had his detective demeanor on. "Keisha, had you ever met her? If not, why did you let her in the door?"

She thought about it. "No, but I talked to her a couple of times when she called and Kelly was out. And Kelly told me how worried she was about Janice Balcomb. I just assumed she'd come to talk about Sandra Balcomb and what we could do together. Guess I'm gullible and always believe the best of people."

And that, I thought, was one of the reasons I loved Keisha.

It was after five when everyone left but the house was clean and the food put away. I headed for a nap. We still had a wedding coming up.

****

I sort of intended that nap to be the end of my day, but it was far from over. I had totally forgotten that Keisha was spending the night in the apartment so that she and José wouldn't see each other the next day. It tickled me that she was so invested in the wedding superstitions of an earlier day.

She and José arrived in a large bit of drama about eight, just as we finished breakfast for dinner—mostly leftovers supplemented by scrambled eggs and bacon, all either one of us felt like doing, though Maggie did say, "We've had a lot of breakfast today."

Keisha bustled in carrying a dress wrapped in a dark plastic thing that stores put expensive dresses in—no chance that anyone could see it before. José carried a suitcase—no, not an overnighter but one that looked like she would be traveling for a week. He took it out to the apartment, but she wouldn't let him near the dress. I guess she thought he'd peek. José actually looked a little tired—but then, it had been a long day, from kidnapping and rescue through bridal shower. We were all a little worn—except Keisha who was lit up like a light bulb.

She poured herself a glass of red wine and asked José if he wanted a beer, which he declined. Apparently she'd already forgotten her vow never to drink wine again. Then she sat and went through the plans for tomorrow, essentially giving each of us our orders. The wedding was scheduled for four in the afternoon, so we had the morning free—if she could be contained—but we were to have her and the girls at the Grill, fully dressed by three-thirty. They would hide in the small anteroom between the ladies room and Peter's office. José was to get there, with his family, no later than three-forty-five—not one minute later. Mike and I, I supposed, were to deliver her and the girls and stay there.

The band and the minister would also arrive at three-forty-five, with Keisha's family, and Mona would set up her stand outside about four. That worried me more than a bit—it was in the forties tonight, with strong winds predicted for the next day and a high of fifty. I crept away to call Mona but she said not to worry—she and Peter had worked out a kitchen arrangement. What blessed friends we had!

Finally, close to ten, José said, "Babe, I have to go. Got to get some sleep." He turned to Mike. "No more surprises tonight, okay?"

"I hope not," Mike said fervently.

Keisha threw her arms around him and said, "Tomorrow, baby, tomorrow!"

He kissed her and made a hasty exit. We shepherded Keisha out to the apartment, not that she was tired, but we were.

"Mom, can I sleep in the apartment with Keisha tonight?" Maggie had an earnest look, and I wondered a bit about the motivation behind this. Was she curious about a bride's thoughts on her wedding night?

Em chimed in. "Me, too. Please?"

I looked at Keisha, who said. "I'm not ready to go to sleep. I'd be pleased to have them for company."

So once more, we carried pallets out to the apartment. The girls got into pajamas and brushed their teeth in the house, and, kissing us goodnight, headed out to the apartment. Mike and I watched until they were safely inside and then stood enveloped in a big hug.

"Let's go to sleep," he said, and we did. Asleep instantly, both exhausted.

We were still asleep at daylight, which comes late in January, when Mike's phone rattled us both to consciousness. I heard him mumble, "Shandy," and then explode, "What the hell? How did that happen?"

Every muscle in my body tensed with foreboding, though I didn't know of what. Davis and Buxton were in jail, Sanford was not but was too milquetoast to try anything, Jo Ellen was safely institutionalized.

"When?" Mike asked tersely. Then, "Oh dear God, I'll be there right away. I assume there's an APB out. Put a guard on my house, the Balcombs, and get José in there—he'll be safer there than in his apartment. Oh, and stake out the Old Neighborhood Grill. Should be empty at this point but keep watch."

My heart sank. It wasn't over, though I couldn't imagine what had happened. Mike leaned back into the bed and wrapped his arms around me. "Jo Ellen escaped from the facility in Vernon. Sometime in the night. No telling where she is. You heard me. There'll be a guard on the house. Get Keisha and the girls...and all of Keisha's stuff...inside."

"Will there be a wedding?" I asked with a quaver in my voice. I didn't think I could bear Keisha's disappointment if the ceremony had to be postponed.

"I'll do everything in my power to see that there is," he said. He dressed quickly—full uniform—and said he'd get the girls and Keisha in on his way out.

I lay in bed, contemplating the last few minutes of peace that I had and yet not comfortable. Fear was back to haunt me.

The girls fussed, didn't want to eat, didn't know what they wanted, but they were irritable...and scared. We saw the police car in front and the officer patrolling the house, yard and apartment. It was reassuring but not completely. The girls asked over and over if they could still go to the wedding.

Keisha was the only one of us upbeat. "Sure you can, sweeties. Ain't nothin' or nobody gonna stop this wedding."

Mike called about ten to report a body had been found on 287, the highway from Vernon through Wichita Falls to Fort Worth. A man, dressed in work clothes, shot once in the head. Identification had apparently been quick and easy—he was a Vernon businessman headed to Fort Worth for Monday appointments, wallet still in his pocket. The shocked family finally managed to say he'd been driving a 2012 silver Camry, and they even gave license plates.

Mike had no doubt that it would all be over quickly and that the poor gentleman had just picked up the wrong hitchhiker, Jo Ellen North, who was now driving a silver Camry. Patrol cars and helicopters were watching not only 287 but back roads into Fort Worth. She'd never make it, he assured me.

Somewhat reassured, I hung up the phone, repeated Mike's optimistic report, and announced we were having breakfast. Keisha made omelets—darn! Why could she do all those things I can't?—while I roasted bacon in the oven, made toast, and set out butter and jam. Wouldn't you know? I burned the bacon. But not too badly. Nobody said anything.

By almost one o'clock, we still hadn't heard anything. Mike called just before one to report they simply hadn't found her. She'd disappeared down back roads no one could find in spite of a multi-county alert—state troopers, county sheriffs, everyone was on the lookout for her. It was, I decided, time to pray.

At two-thirty, Mike told us to proceed with our plans, so Keisha went out to get her dress and suitcase, and we began dressing in the house, with me glancing out the window every so often. Two police officers were now marching around the house.

About three, Keisha emerged from the girls' bathroom,

resplendent in the wedding gown none of us had seen. It was yards and yards of white chiffon billowing everywhere with great random patches of color, principally the turquoise of Maggie's dress and the pink of Em's. Keisha herself was radiant; she and the girls together were a symphony of color. I insisted they pose for a photo, wondering to myself just a bit if this was the last photo I'd ever take of them. *Stop it, Kelly!*

My dress paled in comparison. It was a soft rosy beige, loose enough to hide my belly bump, with a full-length matching cardigan over it. The girls exclaimed about how pretty, and I pretended to believe them. I did put on a bit of extra makeup, especially a bolder lipstick than I usually wore. We were all dressed up for a party and nowhere to go.

Mike called again. The patrol at the house would escort us to the Grill, and another car with one officer would replace them at the house, just to be sure. So, when every instinct was to duck, I boldly led my entourage to the driveway and into the police car—one officer got left behind because we wouldn't all fit.

We set off for what I hoped would be a festive and safe occasion.

Chapter Nineteen

When we drove into the Grill parking lot, the officer suddenly said, "Ladies, get on the floor of the car, please. Now!"

The urgency in his voice needed no more emphasis, and we all dove for the floor though not before I, sitting in the front seat, saw a silver Camry parked across the lot from the Grill. The officer—why I had never learned his name?—talked softly but urgently on his two-way whatever and I thought I heard Mike on the other end, saying, "Blast and damn!"

"Stay down, ladies. Help will be here in a minute."

And it was. Four police cars, sirens blaring, lights blazing, roared into the parking lot.

We crouched on that floor for hours—or so it seemed. Keisha, in the back seat between the girls and no doubt wrinkling her gorgeous dress, muttered, "Some wedding day." My right thigh began to cramp until I thought I'd cry out in pain, and Em whimpered, drawing closer to Keisha. Maggie reached an arm around to comfort her but remained stoic herself.

The police officer driving the car neither ducked nor cringed but kept us informed—"Police checking all cars in parking lot and across the street." Then, "Police going into café…." A short time later we all heard the sirens as an ambulance pulled up to the door of the Grill. "Medics going inside," our informer said, and my heart pounded in my chest. *Peter. Please God, not Peter!*

The medics came out a short time later, leading a dazed but walking Peter. They checked him thoroughly and allowed him back in the building. But the ambulance pulled around the building and parked at the side.

"Ladies, we have the high sign. You may go into the restaurant, but I'm to drive you to the door and escort you in."

Painfully, we crept back to our seats and stretched cramped muscles as he drove the few feet to the door. A police officer was on either side of the door, looking not at us but scanning the surroundings with an intensity that was frightening. We hustled inside, to find Peter sitting forlornly at one of the front tables, holding his head.

"Are you all right?" I asked, rushing toward him.

"Barely. She really hit me hard, and my headache is fierce."

Without another word, Keisha began to massage his scalp and neck. "Get some hot tea," she snapped at me.

I knew the restaurant well enough to find the tea bags and a cup and get hot water out of the spigot on the coffee pot. Peter sipped, and I could see him relax even as I watched his every move and expression.

"What happened?" I asked.

"She caught me in my office, hit me with the butt end of a pistol. Hard. I'm not sure after that, but I think when the officers arrived she ran out my secret back door."

Completely irrelevantly, I asked, "You have a secret back door?"

He nodded. "I never let anyone in my office, so no one knows. Don't you ladies tell." And a bit of the old Peter smile came back.

Just then we heard gunshots—three quick ones, a pause, and then just one. We froze, but it wasn't too long before Mike came in.

"Jo Ellen North is dead," he announced.

Cheering wasn't appropriate, nor was rejoicing in a death, any death. But I felt a great sense of relief. "What happened?"

"She ran for the railroad tracks, but when she saw how close we were, she turned and fired. Shots went wild except she nicked one of our guys in the shoulder. Another took her out with one well-placed bullet. She never knew what hit her. And I guess she never knew she'd lost."

I cried. For some inexplicable reason, I couldn't stop crying. Em and Maggie hugged me, offered me napkins from the dispenser on the table. And I kept crying—for Jo Ellen, who'd made such a mess out of her life because of greed, for her father who'd made a mess out of his life out of love. For all of us caught up in this sordid tale—except maybe Mrs. Buxton and Greg Davis. It was Keisha who brought me out of it.

"Listen up, people," she said in an authoritative voice. "No one knows about all this but us. Most of the police vehicles will disappear before people get here. This is my wedding day, and by God, neither Jo Ellen North nor anyone else is going to ruin it. You put on your happy faces, smile, laugh, dance. Celebrate with me. Please?"

****

And celebrate we did. I ushered Keisha, Maggie and Em into the small anteroom between Peter's office (now blocked off by crime scene tape) and the ladies restroom, took a minute to refresh my makeup, and then went out to meet and greet.

The band showed up—a bass guitar, a fiddle player, and a sax player. I had feared a harmonica player and was much relieved. As guests arrived, the young men played a variety of tunes, from patriotic to African American to who knows what—"This Land is Your Land," "Go

Tell It on the Mountain," "Kumbaya," "Michael, Row the Boat Ashore," even "We Shall Overcome." And they were good. They had me tapping my feet and clapping in rhythm. Who knew Keisha had such talented cousins?

Our extended family began to arrive, along with Keisha's family—her mom, sister, nieces and nephews. The uncle who was to perform the ceremony greeted me like a long-lost friend.

Behind the counter, Peter, dispensing drinks, appeared his usual happy self and when I whispered a question about his head, he said, "Maybe Keisha should go into physical therapy. After her massage, my head feels just fine."

"No," I retorted, "I need her in my office."

We grinned and high-fived.

José and his parents arrived, followed shortly by a breathless Mike who had run home to change into civilian clothes and looked dashing for his role of escorting the bride.

The ceremony began not too long after four—in view of all that had happened, I considered that a miracle. To the strains of *Ode to Joy*, carried by the sax player, Em did that slow hesitation walk—oh, how we'd practiced—from the ladies room to the front room to stand on the far side of the minister, followed by Maggie who looked frighteningly grown up, and then the crowd stood as Mike escorted Keisha to the front of the restaurant. People from the second room crowded into the first, looked through the large see-through window, and jammed the doorway.

Keisha was simply stunning, and José's eyes were wide with admiration and love. Yes, the minister did ramble, but he finally got to the part where he asked, "Who giveth this woman" and Keisha boldly said, "I give myself to this man." A ripple of laughter, applause, amusement, whatever. And then finally after an endless ceremony, the minister pronounced them man and wife, and José gave his bride a tentative kiss. She would have none of that but threw herself at him for a passionate kiss that lasted—well, if not minutes, several seconds. The band played the traditional recessional from *Midsummer Night's Dream.* They must have practiced it repeatedly because they did a good job.

All of us gathered to witness this were stunned into silence and then broke into furious applause.

Without us knowing it, Mona had arrived with supplies for the hot dogs and set up shop in the kitchen. When the joy died down, the band continued its wide selection, and people began to wander up to the counter. Mona had brought a whiteboard with her choices on it—not all that she offered at Bun Appetit, but a good number. People laughed, sang, toasted the bride and groom, danced when they could find space in the small restaurant, and had a wonderful time. It was the happiest wedding I've ever been to, and I even put Jo Ellen, Greg Davis, and Mrs. Buxton out of my mind.

I ran out of steam by six o'clock and began to fear that José and Keisha would dance all night, but they soon left in the 1980s Ford pickup that José had restored. Someone had written "Newlyweds" on the back window and done the old-fashioned trick of tying tin cans to the back bumper, so that they rattled away in a storm of bouncing cans, lots of shouts of "Good luck," and a threat or two of a shivaree. I suspected the young people in the group—mine, Anthony's, and maybe Claire's—were responsible for the car decorations.

After they rounded the corner on Eighth Avenue, a subdued group trooped inside. I sank against Mike and let him support me.

"Tired?"

"Beyond that," I replied.

He gathered the girls who were reluctant to leave, we thanked Peter and Mona for a wonderful event, and we headed home. It was good to be in a quiet house with just my family.

We didn't talk much after we got home, but I did ask Mike how Jo Ellen had escaped and gotten a gun. He almost but not quite chuckled. "I imagine there's one guard at the prison in Vernon who's losing his job. He was found locked in Jo Ellen's cell without his gun. I have no idea how she did it, but she was clever. We all know that."

I collapsed back on the bed, but now sleep didn't come easily. From tomorrow on, I was going to be primarily a mom. I swear I felt the baby kick as I thought that, and then my mind wandered on how far we had come from our first encounter with Jo Ellen North. Then I was a struggling, single mom of two in a house I hated, building a business I feared would collapse any day. Now I had a family—a husband, two daughters growing up too fast to suit me, a new baby on the way, the house of my dreams, and a large extended family. Plus a business that was doing well. Truly I was blessed.

Oh sure, I'd still worry about my beloved Fairmount, preserving its charm, keeping it safe. But I had a feeling Keisha would take on those responsibilities with delight.

I turned over, cuddled close to Mike and slept.

THE END

ABOUT JUDY ALTER

An award-winning novelist, Judy Alter is the author of six books in the Kelly O'Connell Mysteries series: *Skeleton in a Dead Space, No Neighborhood for Old Women, Trouble in a Big Box, Danger Comes Home, Deception in Strange Places,* and *Desperate for Death.* She also writes the Blue Plate Café Mysteries—*Murder at the Blue Plate Café, Murder at the Tremont House,* and *Murder at Peacock Mansion.* The Oak Grove Mysteries debuted in 2014 with *The Perfect Coed*, and Judy plans a sequel.

Her work has been recognized with awards from the Western Writers of America, the Texas Institute of Letters, and the National Cowboy Museum and Hall of Fame. She has been honored with the Owen Wister Award for Lifetime Achievement by WWA and inducted into the Texas Literary Hall of Fame.

Judy is retired as director of TCU Press and the mother of four grown children and the grandmother of seven. She and her Bordoodle, Sophie, live in Fort Worth, Texas.

Follow Judy at www.judyalter.com, Judy's Stew or on Facebook at https://www.facebook.com/pages/Judy-Alter-Author/366948676705857